I0601246

CLEO BROWNE

Tuesday

Devil's Rose MC Book Five

This book was professionally typeset on Reedsy.
Find out more at reedsy.com

Contents

Trigger Warnings

This book deals with badassery in all its forms.
Please be aware that in order for these characters to be badass,
this book contains content that some readers may find
disturbing,
such as graphic descriptions of violence and torture, and R18
sex scenes.

Hey Readers!

Well, I'm sure nobody thought Chewy would get another book,
and yet here we are!
When my buddies Michelle Dups and Nat Logan (yes, that was a
humble brag) suggested how fun it'd be to watch Chewy
become a mom, well, I couldn't help but think "hell yeah!"
even if it did throw out my plan a little.
But hey, what's a messed up plan when I get to revisit the
woman who kicked started this whole thing?
So anyhoo, here's to Michelle and Nat for the good idea. I owe
you one!

Who the heck is that?

Devil's Rose MC

Marx – Pres

Rhodie – VP and Enforcer + Tuesday Tombs (Chewy) Icer

Rider – SAA

Wire – Secretary/Hacker + Remy Wright

Jovie (Wire and Remy's adopted child)

Tank – Member + Mira (Doll) Campbell

Switch – Medic

Judge – Member

Sniper – Member

Fox – Member

Nitro – Member

Savage – Member (ex Death Rider) + Nat

= Rosie

Dex – Member (Ex Death Rider)

TumTum (Jimmy) – Member

Chef (Takoda) – Member

Tav – Member + Blanche (Pixie)

= Niko, Sage, Cove, Elio, Tess

Niko – Prospect

Tombs Security

August (Gus) Tombs + Ana Tombs
= Jr (Sidney)
Jules Tombs + Violet Davies
= Juno
Tav Tombs + Blanche Landry
= Niko, Sage, Cove, Elio, Tess
Tuesday (Chewy) Tombs + Rhodie
= Laney-May
Sidney (Pops) Tombs + Debs Taylor (Mother of Ana)

Bartashev Bratva

Roman Bartashev + Sasha Bartashev (BFF's of Ana)

Prologue

Rhodie

Fuck I love it when Chewy does that thing with her tongue. She's so fucking perfect and always horny for me, especially after "dispatching" the bad guys.

"Fuck, yes baby, just like that, don't stop," I hiss out.

She grins up at me, whiskey eyes sparkling, my cock pressing obscenely against the side of her cheek before she sucks me down again. I let her pump my shaft with her hand, her tongue working me over for two more pumps, fuck it, maybe three, before I yank her off, my hands holding her under her arms, lifting her until she's hovering over my hard cock.

"Line me up baby, I want to cum in your tight pussy,"

"Aye, aye captain!" She salutes, gripping me in her small fist.

She rubs the crown of my cock through her dripping folds, the little tease, before I feel her sink down, impaling me in her wet heat. We both groan, Chewy's head lolling back on her shoulders as she pumps her legs, rising and falling, her large breasts bouncing in rhythm. Watching her like this, taking her pleasure, is one of my favorite things to do. Watching her sleep, and maim people, come a close second and third.

She opens her eyes, staring at me, gifting me her gaze before her lips tilt and she leans back, resting her hands on my calves so she's stretched out riding me. Moving my hand from her soft hip I rest it behind my head, relaxing back as I enjoy the view of my ol lady's pussy. Her plump lips spread wide around my cock, her cream running down my shaft, her clit swollen and proud, begging me to work it just the way she likes. Leaning up I let a string of saliva fall onto her candy pink nub, before resuming my position, one hand behind my head, the other flat against her stomach, my thumb gliding from the base of my shaft, collecting a little more of her wetness to join my spit on her pussy as I rub her clit.

Chewy lets out a whimper and her thighs start to shake, so I know she's close. I flick her clit before pinching it and she explodes around me, flooding me with her release, her screams of pleasure bouncing off the walls. She's glorious like this, hair wild, body shaking, whimpering. All because of me. Sitting up I gently run my hands up her sides, wrapping my arms around her, pulling her into my chest. Pressing kisses to her temple I let her flop against me as I gently rock my hips, my cock sliding slowly in and out of her quivering pussy.

"I can't take anymore," Chewy breathlessly moans, but she tells lies. She's rocking back against me, her hips matching my rhythm.

"Give me one more baby, one more and I'll cum with you," I whisper, hooking some of her curls behind her ear, exposing the sensitive place on her neck where I lay a kiss.

"I want your cum Rhodie. Please, I need it. I need you." she whines, circling her hips.

I know what she's searching for. I know all her needs and

what will set her off. She doesn't need slow, gentle love making right now. She needs to be fucked. I run my hands down her back, gripping her perfect, plump ass. Spreading her cheeks wide I ram up into her, relishing the squeal she makes, her face pressed against my jaw.

"Just like that! Yes, baby, please!" she begs.

I do it again. And again and again. My grip on her ass is punishing as I buck up into her hot slick core. She begins to shake in my arms, and I marvel every time how fucking responsive she is, how sensitive she is and how much she loves to be fucked every which way. The base of my back starts to tingle, my balls pulling up tight ready to blow and, as if her body can read mine, her pussy clamps down, her muscles milking the cum right out of my balls as I shoot my release into her.

Pressing kisses to her cheek, her jaw, her neck, anywhere she's exposed, we come down together, still joined as she relaxes on my chest.

"Psst, what are you thinking about?" Chewy says in her normal voice. I have no idea why I ever expect her to whisper.

I think for a moment. Chewy loves to know what I'm thinking. And it can't be "nothing" or something mundane. If it is, she'll pester me until I think of something more interesting.

"Just thinking about how responsive your body is to mine. How much I love your tight, wet pussy. That sort of stuff." I shrug, her body moving with mine. "What are you thinking?"

"Just about the Manwitch." She says, a finger playing with my chest hair as her head rests between my shoulder and jaw.

"You mean that shit he said about me having a daughter and she's waiting for you to find her?"

"Yeah. That."

I move slightly so I can see her face. "Babe, I have no clue

3

what the fuck he was on about. Dude is weird as hell. Besides, I thought you didn't believe in his visions?"

She scrunches up her face, "Usually pattern recognition is all it is. But I've researched it and there is no way he could have pattern recognition good enough to find Vi out of nowhere. So what if he *does* have some type of magic juju?"

"Magic juju?" I ask, my brow raising.

"Well, what would you call it? It's clearly not science." Her brows pinch, "Unless it is and I haven't researched enough fringe experiments, maybe?" she says more to herself, than to me.

"Well, we both know that we don't have a kid out there. You know I don't have any kids anywhere."

"As far as you know," she adds.

I roll my eyes, "Fine, as far as I know." I better fucking not. I refuse to be Jules Tombs part II. "Besides, are we doing kids? Or are we just Chomper type people?"

She looks up at me, squinting a little as she holds my gaze. "Are you saying that because you think I'd be a bad mom to human kids?"

I let out a sigh, "Babe, you are the most stubborn person I know. You learn at the speed of light and when you put your mind to shit, you always excel. You're the perfect gator mom and all round good person. If you want to be a mom one day then I know, in my soul, that you'd be an awesome mom." I press a kiss to her forehead believing every fucking word I said.

A small smile plays on her lips and she burrows closer to me, her hands folded and tucked under her chin, like little T Rex arms.

"You're my person, Rhodes Paxton."

"And you're mine, Tuesday Tombs."

Chapter 1

Chewy

"**M**iss, can you please stop tapping," The reception lady asks, her brows pinched with what I'm guessing is irritation, staring at my right hand rhythmically tapping out a beat.

"I would like to say yes, but I'm unsure. Sometimes my fingers have a mind of their own."

Her frown deepens and I know that I have most definitely irritated her. "Why are you still here? I told you that I can't send you through to see Sergeant Davies without you stating what your business is."

My left brow pulls in, which is new, they usually both move at the same time. I'll investigate that later. Right now I need to get away from this reception desk. It smells weird and the nonstop ringing phones will give me a headache if I have to keep standing here.

"That is untrue. I believe you asked me what my business was and I told you that I declined to answer your question. It's between Davies and I."

She lets out a long sigh, rolling her eyes and I think I may be wearing her down. "Is he expecting you?"

I stare at her, making eye contact so she knows I'm serious. "Just tell him Tuesday Tombs is here to see him."

She gives me a suspicious look. I know that one from my flashcards. It's kinda side squinty with a pinched mouth. Although it's hard to tell because this woman has had a pinched unhappy mouth this whole conversation. She presses a button on her phone, gives me a funny look then swivels around in her chair so I can't stare at her. Or hear her conversation. Joke's on her, I have phenomenal hearing. She places the phone down, stares at me and then shuffles some papers. Before I can complain Moss catches my eye, walking purposefully down the hall toward us.

"Tuesday, good to see you. You wanted to speak with me?" He stands in front of me, and I dart my eyes around the foyer I'm standing in.

"Can we go somewhere private? Oh, maybe an interrogation room? I haven't been in one at this station."

Moss's brows jump up, "But you've been in them in other stations?"

"Of course I have."

He shakes his head, then gestures to follow him. But we don't get anywhere near an interrogation room. Instead he leads me to what must be his desk. It's tidy, and there's a picture of two little boys which I'm guessing are his twins. I don't know much about them, other than someone mentioned he has them and he's a single dad. I never asked because I didn't care, but now I'm wondering if perhaps I should mention them now. He gestures to a chair and I've missed my chance. Shrugging, I look around the room and I don't like how everything is situated.

6

"The furniture in this room is terribly organized." I frown at a desk sitting at a 70 degree angle to his with no rhyme or reason.

He gives me a puzzled look, before looking around, "I guess. It's always been like this."

"Well, I don't care for it. I'm going to move this desk a little before I can sit down." I do exactly that, the legs of the desk making an awful screeching noise as I drag it further from Moss's desk, and spinning it slightly so it sits flush against the wall, not jutting out of it into Moss's space. "There." I clap my hands, then take a seat.

"Well, thanks for that," Moss says drily, "So, what brings you here?"

"I need your help."

"OK. In what way?"

I squint at him a little, running my plan through my mind once more, looking for kinks. Finding none, I hit Moss with a look. "I need you to accompany me to find Rhodie's daughter."

He leans back in his chair. "You mean the daughter that neither of you know about? The one the Manwitch spoke of? I thought you didn't believe in his visions?"

I don't usually, however, what he said hit a nerve. Never once did I think that we would have children. Not for any real reason other than I'm very busy. But once the seed was planted I saw how Rhodie interacted with the MC kids. He's a good man and good with children. He's patient and kind, he listens to them and respects their thoughts and feelings. Rhodie is the very best of men and he deserves to help raise a good human just like him.

"I didn't. But I can't explain how he knew where to find Violet or the children. Trust me, I've looked into everything."

"Right. So because of lack of evidence you believe an ex-

Bratva who has visions and you need my help to find a child that apparently belongs to you and Rhodie." I nod in reply. He's cleverer than I thought. "How will you know which child is your one?"

"Not sure. But the Manwitch was confident, and so am I." I move to stand. "So, are you coming?"

"I kinda have a job here, Chewy."

My eyes flick to the giant clock on the wall. "You clock off in half an hour. I've already arranged things with your family. They will take care of your twins. This won't take long."

He stares at me, perhaps in shock. I'm not overly sure. "You rearranged my whole life to get me to come on a crazy mission to find a child you know nothing about and you want to leave in 30 minutes?"

"Exactly!" I grin at him.

He starts spluttering, moving papers across his desk, huffing a little. "You can't be serious and expect me to drop everything."

"Yes I can. Candice Rogers will be there."

He freezes, the only thing moving are his eyes as they turn to look at me. "Am I bringing her in?"

"Nope."

He blinks. Once, twice. "Well, when you say it like that, I think I can free up some time."

Rhodie

It's been a long fucking day and I'm glad that the little cabin Chewy and I live in is far enough away from the garage that I get a good ride home. Riding my sled, the wind blowing through my hair, is the very best way to get rid of the bullshit of the day. If that wasn't fucking blissful enough, knowing that I'll be going home to my woman is the fucking cherry on top.

I pull into the long drive, idling down it until I stop outside our cabin. Kicking down the stand, I throw my leg over and then stomp my way up the little front steps. As per usual the door is unlocked when I turn the handle and walk through it. For someone that works in security, Chewy really is relaxed about the security in her own home. Although I guess having her home nestled between her brothers and Pops probably helps.

"Babe? You here?"

I knock on the kitchen island as I walk past, looking for my woman. The most perfect woman in the world, a woman made just for me. Yeah, shes fucking quirky and perhaps a bit unhinged, but fuck it, she's mine and I love her.

"Babe?"

I look through the spare bedroom, and the bathroom, finding the house empty. Huh. That's weird.

She would have finished work by now so I'm guessing she's at the clubhouse. She's been working like a woman possessed on finding that Happy Values bitch, Candice, so I'm sure she's in Wire's domain doing her thing. I slam the door shut behind me, mount my ride and pull out. I mean, getting more wind therapy time is always a good thing. My eyes scan the road as I head through town. The nights are warmer with summer on the way and soon the streets will be filled with kids on summer break. Rose Grove is a cozy town that draws families in. In the summer there are packs of kids hanging out with their friends at the Square, or even at the swimming pool. There's rivers young people like to head off to and parents trust that the town is safe.

To an extent it is, the DRMC will keep it as safe as we can, but we'd all feel a fuck ton better getting rid of Candice Rogers once and for all.

Pulling into the clubhouse I raise a chin at Niko. TumTum still mans the gate, even after getting his patch, but on certain days he takes one for the team and lets Niko sit out there. I smirk to myself as I park up. No prospect likes gate duty, it's the shittiest of all the jobs we hand out, and yet TumTum loves it. Go figure.

"Hey brother," Tank lifts his chin as he leads the way into the clubhouse.

"Yo, how's things?"

"Fucking amazing," Tank grins, beelining for his woman who, as usual, is parked up at a table, laptop at the ready.

I slap him on the back, fucking happy for him. He used to be quiet, reserved and not unhappy, but not the best version of himself that I see now. As opposed to Judge who has been in one hell of a fucking mood since storming out of the diner two months ago. Shrugging off the thought, I head for the Computas.

"Yo babe - fuck!" I spin, covering my eyes, avoiding looking at Wire's ass pumping away.

"Shit! What do you want?!" Wire growls, and hell, I would too if I was interrupted.

A year or so ago I wouldn't have thought anything of seeing a brother fucking anyone. Hell, we used to all fuck in the common room during our wild parties. Then the brothers started falling and now we've all become far more aware about giving each other privacy. Mainly because no one wants their ass beat.

"Sorry, Remy," I apologize. Fuck Wire, he should have known to take that shit to the private side of his suite. I also vow to never sit in either of their chairs. "Just looking for my woman."

"Um, I haven't seen her today," Remy's soft voice answers.

"What?" I spin around, thankfully Remy is sitting primly in her chair as Wire has his unbuttoned jeans pulled up, and is scowling at me.

"I saw her earlier today, but she said she was working on something," Wire grumbles.

"What time was that?"

"Around 3?"

I turn and head for our room, bursting through the door. The room is empty, looking exactly as we left it, except for the open wardrobe door with her go bag missing. The go bag she uses on missions with her brothers. Her brothers who are in the common room with their women as we speak. I take a deep breath, but it does little to calm me. The memories of the first and last time she left me flood my memory. My feet move of their own accord, not stopping until I'm standing in the middle of the common room, surrounded by my family. But not the one person who completes me.

"Yo, has anyone seen Chewy?"

"She mentioned something about having an errand to run," Ana says, rocking Chomper in his stroller.

"What kind of errand? Did she say where she was going?" My voice rises and I just know that something is wrong.

Jules is busy messing around on his phone, and I know that something isn't quite right. "Why the fuck is she headed toward Roxburgh?"

"What the fuck?! She never said anything about leaving town. Her phone is off and her go bag is gone." I scrub my hands through my hair. Why the fuck would she be going there? Fucking Pops, I bet he has something to do with this. "Pops!" I bellow.

"Keep your hair on kid. Shit! What's your problem?" Pops growls.

"Fuck, you're here. I figured it was some bullshit idea you came up with." Fuck. If he's here she's on her own somewhere. Which is fucking dangerous as she has a habit of offering herself up to be kidnapped.

"Gee, thanks asshole." Pops rolls his eyes.

I scrub my hands through my hair, trying to ignore the looks Gus and Jules share.

"She's hunting," Jules says aloud, Gus nodding in agreement.

"Yesssss," Vi says under her breath, a little fist pump action going on. "What?" she asks, wide-eyed.

My fists clench and unclench. What the hell is she thinking? She doesn't need to do this shit, that's what I'm here for. How the fuck am I meant to protect her if she does this? I blow out a breath, aiming my gaze at the men who are my brothers-in-law. "Tell me where she is, I need to get to her, what if she needs help?"

"I saw Moss leave with her," one of Vi's sisters says, looking confused over what's happening.

"What the actual fuck!?"

Before I can demand that someone call Moss, the other sister holds up her hand. "His phone is off, too."

My big brother stands in the doorway, hands on hips, watching the whole scene go down. He turns to look at Jules, "How long do you let her hunt before you step in?"

"She knows to check in after 6 hours. Then 12, 18, and 24. If we haven't heard from her we go in," Tav answers.

"Well, let's let her hunt," Marx says, nodding.

What the fuck? No, Pres or not that's a shit call. "But-"

"No buts, brother. Your woman is dangerous and she knows

12

how to do this. Her methods are a little unorthodox," My brows raise because that's a fucking understatement. "but she always gets results. You need to trust her, brother." Marx says, staring me in the eye.

The fight starts to leave my body. He's right. She's all those things and so much more. "Fuck I know all that, but she doesn't need to hunt anymore, she has me to do it for her."

"We love when our big, strong men do things for us, but sometimes we like to do it for ourselves," Ana says. "Chewy is more than capable of doing this, Rhodie. Trust her. Besides, if she's left you here, it's for a reason."

My shoulders slump under the weight of Chewy being out there on her own, and yet I know that what they all say is true. Chewy is fucking special, so for this moment I will trust her. But mark my words, I will be tanning that plump ass of hers when she gets home.

Chapter 2

Chewy

"OK, so once we get there I need you to keep an eye on everything from Truck Norris, got it?"

Moss side eyes me from the passenger seat. "Why do you call this Truck Norris when it's a van?"

"It's an homage to a badass. And there were no good van puns," I reply, keeping my eyes on the road and my hands at ten and two.

"What about Jackie Van?"

I roll my eyes. "That's terrible. There's no imagination in that at all."

"Riiiight."

We travel in silence for a while and I'm starting to have a bit of a funny tummy. Not the poops or anything, more a little clenchy. I have a feeling it's because I've left Rhodie to do this on my own. I probably should have said something, but then he'd be all up in my business and this is something I need to do on my own. Besides, it wouldn't be a surprise if I asked him to come with me.

When the Manwitch called with Candice Rogers' location and where to find Rhodie's daughter I had to drop everything to get on the road. Rhodie would have tried to talk me out of it, but people need closure. Especially Vi. I like her, and this is something I can do to help her get over the trauma. Or something.

Pulling over to the curb, I idle outside the address I was given. It looks exactly like the type of place I expected. Hard architectural lines, stark white, surrounded by concrete and strategically placed cacti. Boring.

"So I sit here on surveillance duty?" Moss asks, turning to peer into the back of Truck Norris.

I clamber between the two front seats into the back space, flicking on the three laptops and the screens connected to them as I make my way to the back.

"Yup. I've already hacked her cameras. See?" I point to six mini screens that have visuals of both the outside and inside of Candice's house.

Moss lets out a low whistle. "Has anyone ever told you you're like, scary good at this stuff?"

I take in the impressed look on his face before letting out a sigh, "All the time, buddy."

I collect up my bag and throw it over my shoulder, before climbing back over the front seat, ready to leave. I pause for a moment, staring at the steering wheel, going over my plan in my head. Once I'm satisfied that I've got all my bases covered I nod to myself, open the door and slide out.

"Wait! How will I know you're OK?" Moss asks, reaching to stop the door from slamming.

"Right hand side of the central laptop, there's an earpiece. Put it in, don't breathe through your mouth, and I'll be back soon." I slam the door before he can ask anything else. He's kinda chatty.

Making my way to the front door where I've already disabled the security system, I let myself in. I almost take my shoes off out of habit and then remember that socks aren't very threatening. Taking in my surroundings I choose the best place to sit and wait. Moss' breathing crackles over my ear piece.

"I'm gonna need you to breathe quieter."

Sounds of rummaging fill my ear before it quietens. "Better?"

"Much."

There's silence, and I can feel that he's going to break it any moment now. "Are you sure about this, Chewy?"

"Of course I am. I've run through every scenario."

"Including the one where Rhodie may not be happy that you've run off to find a kid without him?"

Ugh. Why do neurotypical people have to be so good at pointing out that kind of stuff? Yes, I have thought about how upset Rhodie will be, but it will only be for a short period of time. "I have thought about it, but we'll be back in a few hours. Rhodie trusts me."

Moss makes a weird humming noise. "Look, I'm not saying he doesn't trust you, but from what I've seen of the DRMC they don't look like the type of guys who love it when their women go off on missions alone."

"It was only that one time that I went off to save those trafficked women. Oh, and then the time I purposely got kidnapped and came home with a sweet ride. This would make it the third time and then I'm sure it'll be out of my system," I inform Moss. Judging by the chuckling coming through the line, I doubt he believes me.

"If you say so," he replies.

I spin, surveying the seating options. Letting out a sigh I drag a chair into the middle of the room. Far away from anything hard that she may want to bludgeon me with, not that it's likely. I plop down, and think through my plan. Once I have Candice the interrogation will begin. I move my right foot a smidge until I can feel my interrogation go bag with my secret weapon on the floor beside me. I can't question her in the Rev Room just yet. I need answers immediately, then she will be taken back home to be dealt with.

My fingers tap against my thigh, as I stare at the door, my leg jiggling as I wait. My senses are being raped by florals, the smell giving me a headache as I sit in this shitty, hard chair. Why do fancy people have such uncomfortable furniture? Jules used to have uncomfortable furniture too, but now he has Violet and Juno to love so he had to get comfortable stuff. Stuff for families to sit on, closely, maybe even hugging or letting their legs touch or something.

I'll add that to my list of things I need. I have a comfy couch, it's very soft, but it's light colored and that's not family friendly. I type "dark colored soft couch" in my notes app and then turn my phone off.

"Need anything?" Moss's voice calls over the comms after a while.

"Yes. I'll need some coffee grounds to sniff once I get out of here."

"Ooookay," Moss mumbles and I smile to myself.

After rescuing Vi I've seen the sergeant in a different light. Hence why I've brought him with me instead of Rhodie. Rhodie will be all Hulk smashy and I need subtlety. Well, someone more subtle than Rhodie.

I tilt my head when the jingling of keys breaks through the

silent house and I know it's almost showtime. The door opens and a spicy scent cuts through the sickly florals and now all the scents are mingling and making my throat feel thick. I close my eyes and take two breaths, in and out, through my mouth, to refocus.

The light flicks on and I open my eyes to stare at the person I've been hunting for two months now.

"Hello, Candice. I hear you have my Ol Man's daughter."

Rhodie

"So, are you gonna like, sit down and act like a normal person or just pace?" Rider asks, from his position stretched out on the couch.

It's been three hours since the last known sighting of Chewy and I'm antsy as fuck. I tried taking a nap but I could smell her on my pillow and that just twisted my guts up in even tighter knots.

"You know, there was a time when I thought you and every man in here would spend the remainder of your lives working, drinking and fucking. Then you went and fell in love and everyone started falling like dominoes. How does it feel to be pussy whipped?" Rider, the asshole smirks, Fox and Nitro joining in.

I send a glare his way, and ignore the fucker. He loves Chewy just as much as I do.

"What are you so wound up for, anyway, brother?" Sniper asks, leaning forward in his chair, a serious look on his face.

Sniper is one of the more reserved brothers. He and Judge probably had some of the shittiest jobs when we were deployed, and I know that the DRMC is a haven for them. Who the fuck knows where they'd be, mentally and physically without the MC?

I stop pacing, settling my gaze on Sniper. "I always worry about her, she's the other half of me. But this whole Candice thing has me wound tighter than usual. Not to mention what the Manwitch said." I let out a long breath.

"Ah, there it is. The crux of the problem." Nat says, planting her ass in Savage's lap. "Are you worried that she's going after Candice? Or that she could very well come back with a kid?"

My head drops, chin to chest and I let out a sigh. "Can it be both?" I ask, raising my head with a grimace.

"Candice isn't a problem. We all know what Chewy is capable of," Dex answers and what began as me pacing in the common room has turned into an intervention. Or group counseling or some shit.

"Which means Rhodie is afraid of Chewy bringing home a baby," Mira sings.

Chewy's brothers who are sitting quietly at one of the tables all share a look. A suspicious fucking look. So I point it out.

"It was nothing," Tav placates. "Just that we're on your side."

"My side?" I frown, trying to figure out what the fuck he's talking about.

"Yeah, you know, not wanting Dayz to come home with a kid. Can you imagine it? I mean it was bad enough with Jules," Tav jokes, earning himself a scowl from Jules.

"Why don't you want Chewy to come home with a kid?" I turn on him, growling.

He shrugs. "Well, you know how she is. I mean, a gator mom,

sure, but a kid? What's Chewy going to do when she gets locked into work? Who's going to look after it when she's in the Rev Room? What about Chomper? I mean, shit, is she really cut out for that?"

My fists clench at my sides and I have to hold myself back from not only bashing a brother, but also Chewy's brother. "Chewy has so much fucking love in her, you don't even know! Once she puts her mind to shit she can do anything. If she wants us to have this kid then she will be the best goddamn mother you will ever fucking see, so don't talk shit about *my* woman, *your* sister. All you three fuckers, above everyone here should know what Tuesday is capable of."

Gus, Tav and Jules share identical fucking shit-faced grins. When it finally dawns on me that I walked into that one I scrub my hand down my face before rolling my shoulders, letting go of any tension I had been feeling.

"Well, now that you've come to terms with your feelings, sit your ass down and behave like a normal person. Shit kid, you're giving me a fucking headache," Pops grumbles, pulling Mama Debs into his lap.

"You know, there is something we can actually be doing to help you kill the time," Mira offers, from her spot on Tank's lap. Seeing all the women sitting on their men makes me miss mine even more. Maybe Rider is right, I'm utterly pussy whipped. I dig deep to see if I care about that, then came to the realization that nope. I don't care one little bit.

Scrubbing my hand over my face, I think whether I want to ask for Mira's idea or not. The way her and Blanche are grinning at each other is not a good sign, but I guess I'd rather put up with whatever crazy crap they come up with than sit here with my finger up my ass waiting.

"Fine. Tell me what you have in mind."

The next thing I know all the Ol Ladies and Lovely are organizing a car pool, babysitters and a list of some shit or other.

Fuck.

Chapter 3

Chewy

My head beats a gentle pulse and I'm sure my eye is twitching.

"Chewy, I commend what you're doing, but you either need to finish up or kill her because I can't listen to her whining any longer," Moss's voice crackles through the ear piece.

I grunt in reply, not wanting her to know that I have people with me. Lying in wait caught her by surprise and I've been using that to my advantage. However we are now two hours in, she's pissed herself god knows how many times, and between the ugly crying and moments of bravery where she threatens me, she's been whining. Almost nonstop.

"Where are the kids?"

Candice sobs from the chair she's tied to, not even trying to fight her way out. Useless bitch. "I told you, I can't tell you that! Just let me go, please, I won't tell anyone you're here. You're hurting me! My wrists hurt, let me go, you bitch!"

A long, loud sigh leaves my body, "Candice, I really didn't

want to have to do this, but you leave me no choice," I shake my head sadly at her, dragging my backpack closer to where I'm sitting, opposite Candice. In an arm chair that is fucking hard as a rock.

"What more could you do to me?" she whines. "You've already tied me up, I can't even feel my fingers! You cut my hair and ripped off my eyelash extensions, you're a monster!"

"Well, brace yourself, it's gonna get worse for you." I grin as I pull the jar out of my backpack, grinning at Candice's scream and pleas.

"No, no, no, no, no! Get it away from me!" She's squirming in her chair, the cords of her neck showing her effort.

"A little birdy told me you don't like spiders." I hold the jar closer and Candice freezes on the spot, her breathing shallow.

"Tell me what I want to know, and I'll put Hermann away." Yes, I named him Hermann. He's a cute little hairy guy, for a Texas Tan Tarantula.

"I-I-I'll tell you. Just, p-please, p-p-put him away. Please!" There's tears mixing in with her snot and I think I feel sorry for her. No actually, I'm lying. I don't feel sorry for her at all. She made her bed, now she has to lie in it. Which is a weird saying, but I'll think about that later.

I make a show of placing Hermann on the coffee table off to the side of where we're sitting.

"Spill."

* * *

"Good to go?" Moss asks, from his position behind the driver's wheel of Truck Norris.

"Yup. Candice is bagged and tagged and I gave her a little sleepy time juice so she'll be out for a while yet."

He side-eyes me for a moment, "Were you always planning on using the spider?"

"Well, yeah, she has arachnophobia." I shrug, entering the location of the children into GPS. "Fear is one of the best motivators."

"Then why the hell didn't you use it from the get go? I wanted to throw myself in the nearest lake and drown myself listening to her bitch."

"Where's the fun in that?"

Moss lets out a long sigh, "You know what? Let's just find your kid and get out of here. The longer I spend with you, the more sense you make."

I grin in his direction and I see his lips tilt up a little. He's a good-looking guy, but there must be something very wrong with him if his wife left and he's still single. Although he does have kids and I bet that shrivels up people's vagina's. Not all ladies like kids. Or kids that don't belong to them at least. My brows pull in when I realize that Rhodie's child won't be related to me. Or him.

My thumb taps my pinky, then the ring finger, middle, pointer and pinky again, repeating the pattern as I sort through my thoughts. On one hand it's a statistical fact that most child abuse is at the hands of a step-parent. But on the other hand, there are people willing to adopt, or foster, and love children that don't belong to them and they seem to get on fine. Mama Debs isn't related to Ana, or any of us really and I know that she loves us from her actions. Wire and Remy aren't genetically related to Jovie but they love her with all their hearts. Tav isn't

24

related to any of Blanche's kids but they call him dad and he would die for them all. Same as Violet with Juno. The evidence would suggest that many people can successfully love and raise children who don't belong to them.

My finger tapping slows and I feel better about what I'm about to do.

"Are you waiting for backup?" Moss's question pulls me from my thoughts.

Peering through the windscreen I notice Agent Dansen, his SUV and a large van parked on the side of the road. "Oh yeah, I called them when I got the address. They're going to take the kids to be monitored at the hospital and then find their parents."

"What about the kid we're looking for?"

"Manwitch said they'd been in foster care since their parents died. Besides, she has a family waiting for her back in Rose Grove."

He eyes me for a moment before he bobs his head side to side. "Well, I guess if the paperwork is clear, have at it."

"Wait, you're not going to read me my rights or accuse me of kidnapping or something?"

"Would you listen if I did?"

"Not at all."

He snorts. "Then I'd be wasting my time, wouldn't I? Besides, I've seen some shitty parents, and you and Rhodie are not them. You can offer more than I think even you know, Chewy."

I turn to look at him, driving down the dark highway, with the FBI team following us to our destination. "I like you. We're going to be friends."

"I can't think of a better person to have as a friend, Chewy. But maybe stay away from my kids for a few years, I'm not ready to have shit blowing up in my yard just yet."

"It was like, three times, Moss."

"Whatever you say, Chewy." He tries to hide his smile, but I see it.

"Just drive, Moss." My lips tug up and I'm happy to have a new friend.

I'm getting good at this friendship stuff. Motherhood will be a breeze.

Rhodie

This is hell. It has to be. Somewhere between the clubhouse and whatever the fuck this open late big box store is called, I died. I died and went straight to hell. It's the only logical explanation to why I'm following seven Ol Ladies and two of Vi's sisters around pushing a cart that is filled to the brim with small people crap.

"I can't take much more," Rider groans beside me.

"Why the hell are you here anyway? You don't have an Ol Lady dragging you into being here," I frown.

"I came to talk shit at you while you died a little inside. Instead, I'm dying with you. My feet are fucking killing me, and what is all this shit anyway?" He holds up some type of stuffy that looks kinda like an axolotl and a unicorn had a baby before dropping it in disgust.

"Right," Lovely says, her clap drawing my attention, "Because the only thing we know about your child is the fact that she's a girl, we've decided to get one of every age range, and then we can return the stuff she can't fit."

I watch through wide eyes as she throws about 12 little bathrobes into the buggy, all pink, one in each size.

"Ah, Lovely, is that really necessary?"

"Necessary?" Blanche screeches from an aisle somewhere, making both Rider and I jolt. "Is it necessary that the little girl Chewy brings home, a little girl with no family and who has nothing to her name, gets a soft, fluffy bathrobe to fit her?" She moves to stand in front of me, poking her long, bony finger into my chest. "Think about it Rhodie!" she growls through clenched teeth before storming off to a clothing rack within my sight line, grabbing one of every size, and color, while holding my eye contact.

"Blanche! Don't scare him. Rhodie can't help that he's never looked after any of the MC kids because he's always so busy. He doesn't know what all kids need," Mira says helpfully.

Except it's not helpful because she's fucking right. Outside of Chomper, who could probably eat me in my sleep, I've never, not once offered to keep an eye on the kids. I mean I've done school run, but 10 minutes with them strapped into the car and the music blaring is probably not enough experience.

"Uh oh, it's just hit him," Remy whispers, staring at me. Is she holding a dildo?

"No I'm not, you creep!" She swings at me with some nude-colored club.

"Wait, what's hit me?"

"You've just realized that you know nothing about kids." Nat smiles, holding hands with her ol man who has an empty buggy the Ol Ladies are making a beeline for.

I stare at her, give her the look that makes grown men shit their pants and she still doesn't back down. I would argue but she's right. I know nothing about kids. How the fuck am I meant to be a dad?

A large hand lands on my shoulder, giving a tight squeeze. "Go take a walk brother," Savage's blue gaze meets mine, before he gives me a shake and shoves me down the aisle, to walk off whatever the fuck is happening to me.

I wander aimlessly for a while, somehow ending up in an aisle full of little cars, bikes, trucks, and shit that I would have fucking lost my mind for as a kid. I rummage through the Matchbox section, looking through their motorcycle collection.

"You're too old to be here. Are you a perv or something?"

I turn to my right and my eyes land on a chubby ginger kid that looks vaguely familiar. He's wearing a button that reads "Rodney" so I'm guessing that's his name. I stare at him, wondering if I should engage with him or not. He looks about 9 or 10 and even I know kids this age are scary as fuck so it's probably best I ignore him. Clearly he doesn't get that memo before he steps closer, staring up at me, chewing his hot cheetos with an open mouth.

"Perv says what?" he says, around a mouthful.

I frown down at him. "What?"

"Yeah that's what I thought." He flips me his very orange middle finger before scuttling away.

"What in the fuck was that?" I mumble to myself.

Is this the shit I have to look forward to? A kid with a smart mouth and rude finger signs? I let out a long sigh, because yes, that is exactly what I have to look forward to. Rider is my best friend and I just fucking know that he'll teach my kid all that shit and more. Hell, thinking back to our childhood we were fucking awful. I'm amazed my dad didnt kick my ass more. Thinking about Mad Dog I pull out my phone. If I'm having a kid my dad should know.

28

"Yo, son, what's up?"

My whole body settles as soon as my dad's voice rumbles down the line, my lips tilting up. "What? Nothing's up. Can't a son call his dad out of the blue?"

There's a pause on the other end, before a chuckle, "Well, he can, but he doesn't, does he?"

Fuck, he's right, I should make more of an effort to check in. He's been off with his woman for months now, tripping around in his RV. A better son would call regularly. "Yeah, sorry Dad. I should make an effort to check in with you. How are you?" He blows a breath out, and his hesitation makes me worry. "Dad? Is everything OK?"

"Yeah, son, everything is good. I'm on my way home, but minus an Ol Lady. Molly and I decided that we didn't want the same things. And shit, being locked in an RV for days, months on end, we kinda realized that we had nothing in common other than fucking,"

"Fuck, Dad! Don't say shit like that!" His booming laugh comes over the phone and I can't help the smile that tugs at my lips, even though I want to remain grossed out. Forever. "Are you OK with that?"

"Yeah son, it was mutual. She had me drop her at her sisters, and I got the call from your Ol Lady, so I'm making my way home. I know you'll need me.:

My brows fly up. "Chewy called you?"

"Yeah, told me I was going to be a grandpa and to get my ass home. Couldn't come at a better time son."

"So, you're happy?" My stomach flutters knowing that Chewy knew what this would mean to my dad. Shit, to me.

"Fuck yeah! I'm not getting any younger, you know. Besides, that funny little woman of yours would make a good mother. I can't wait to watch her kick the asses of any kid stupid enough to take yours on."

I snort, knowing that's exactly what would happen. "I'm glad you're happy, Dad. I guess I'll see you soon then?"

"Look out your clubhouse window tomorrow, Son. I'll be there."

I rub my chest, feeling the pang there. "Love you Dad."

"Love you too, Son. See you then." Dad's phone clicks off and I feel a renewed energy bubbling up inside me.

I'm going to have a kid. My woman is bringing us home a kid that needs us. My dad will be here and between us, the DRMC, the Tombs and everyone else in our circle we're going to love that kid so hard they'll shit love.

Striding back to where I left the buggy and Ol Ladies I'm taken aback when Blanche comes out of nowhere and shoves a mini-toilet thing into my hands, "Put this in the buggy. And don't bitch." She glares at me and I'm almost happy that Chewy and I are skipping pregnancy because a pregnant Blanche is fucking scary. But her pregnancy rage isn't going to slow me down; I have shit to do to get ready for my family.

Walking toward the buggy with the tiny toilet a kid's voice calls out of nowhere "Nice toilet! Shit much?

"Rodney!"

"Shit! Ms Jasmine!" A fat, orange blur races past me, Vi's sister hot on its heels and a guffaw bursts out of me.

Then I throw my head back and roar.

"Fuck, brothers, that little toilet thing tipped him over the edge," Rider's sad voice breaks through my laughter.

He couldn't be further from the truth. I'm nowhere near the edge. I'm exactly where I should be.

Chapter 4

Chewy

I finally caved and I'm letting Moss lead the way as we quietly make our way through the building Candice said the kids were in. It seems that after the DRMC took down their last place, she's been moving the kids every few days. She's good, I have to give her that. None of these properties show against her name or any of her businesses. Instead, they're all owned by shell companies owned by the shareholders in Happy Values. It's ridiculous the lengths rich people will go to cover their nefarious tracks.

"Hang back, Chewy. I'm going to clear this floor," Moss says in a low voice, his service weapon out in front of him as he stalks down the hall.

I wave him on. I'm fully capable of doing this part, but Moss has been a great side kick so I figured I should let him have some fun. That's how friends work. Sharing is caring and all that crap. Checking my watch I realize that I'm hitting close to six hours away from home, meaning if I don't call or text my brothers, they'll come for me. At this point I really don't need the cavalry so I flick off a quick message.

All going well Moss and I should be back on the road within the next half hour.

"Clear," Moss voices quietly.

I move to stand next to him, looking down the long hall. It's a mansion style house, but instead of the large, white wooden doors you'd expect, each door has a window insert. Peering through I can see a little boy playing with blocks, a woman sitting in a rocking chair, reading a book.

"Looks like each kid has a nanny," Moss murmurs. "There are no guards that I can see, just the women in the rooms with the kids."

I nod, following along, peeking in the windows.

"It's like fucking window shopping. Watch how the kids and nannies pay no attention to us," Moss says with disgust.

I nod in agreement, "Yeah, they've become desensitized."

Moss shakes his head sadly. "How do you know which is your kid?"

There are nameplates on each door, stating the child's name and age. I slowly walk the hall, reading every name on the door until I come to a stop.

Laney–May

2 years old

Moss steps up beside me, before turning wide eyes in my direction. "Roads, Lane," he bobs his head side to side, "May, like the month and the rest of your family names."

A smile tugs at my lips. He cracked it in one. It's what made me stop and pause too. We share a look before peering through the window. There, sitting on the floor, lining up blocks with

32

one hand, the other clasping an alligator stuffy to her chest, is the child I've come here for. Rhodie's child. Rhodie's and *my* child. I wait for a feeling of rightness to come over me, maybe a blooming in my chest, but nothing as of yet.

If I was anyone else I'm sure I'd be concerned, but I'm not. After watching Jules fall in love with his daughter I know that it might take me a little bit of time. Hopefully I'm smarter than Jules and don't need my kid to be almost kidnapped to drive the point home.

Shuffling has my head snapping to the side, my shoulders relaxing when Dansen and his men flood the floor. He looks into a few windows as he makes his way to me and Moss, clocking exactly what we did.

"We'll take the nannies and the children. Did you find the child you were looking for?"

"Yes, I think I have."

Opening the door I walk through, ignoring the nanny jumping up and making a few disgruntled noises, a little shriek leaving her lips when Moss takes control of that situation. I don't care what he does with her, as long as she's far, far away.

"Hello," I say, my head tipped toward the floor, at the mass of brown curls.

Laney-May tips her head back and I'm met with bright green eyes. Just like Rhodie. She says nothing, choosing to stare instead.

"I like your block line. I like to do that, too." Sitting down and picking up a white block, I move it into the correct place, in a straight line, around an inch away from the last block.

She stares at me a moment, then adds on to the line, before looking back at me. I follow her lead and we do this a few more times before she stops, stares and then shuffles closer, sitting her little bottom on my lap. Of their own accord my arms wrap around her, like they do with Chomper, but this time I don't need to avoid a snout.

"You're coming home with me." I then think that might sound bossy, so I add, "If that's OK with you."

I'm not sure if a two year old child understands what I'm saying, or if she can even talk back, but I take her nod as affirmation. The Manwitch said she was ours, so she is.

"Let's go. There's some people you need to meet."

Rhodie

We got the message from Chewy that she's on her way back so instead of going directly home with all the stuff we bought we instead split off. Blanche, who told me she's "nesting" decided to have the only prospect we have meet her at mine and Chewy's cabin so they can build the furniture for the kid. Our kid.

"You gonna be ready for this?" Gus asks, at my side as we walk into the clubhouse after pulling in with more kid shit for our rooms here.

Looking over at the man who will one day be my brother-in-law, I give him my honest answer, "Gus, I have never been ready for anything ever since Chewy blew into my life. The best I can hope for is to hold on tight and ride Chewy's wave because I fucking love that woman, but shit, I'd be lying if I didn't want to tan her ass."

Gus makes a weird growling sound while Tav makes a gagging noise. "Could have gone a lifetime without hearing that."

I grin, slapping him a little too hard on the shoulder before heading to my room to find TumTum and Chef already in there, having unboxed the crib already.

"Boys, let's get this shit done!"

* * *

"What in the fuck is wrong with this thing?" Chef growls in that goddamn panty-melting voice.

"You put the wrong part in! See? Part 1D goes into 16C?" TumTum leans toward Chef, finger pointing at something on the fucking poster sized instruction sheet.

"You better fuck off with that instruction sheet!" Chef tries to snatch the instructions away and there is nothing I can do because I'm having my own mental breakdown trying to figure out this fucking rocking contraption in front of me.

"Rhodie! You better tell him to fuck right off before I shoot him!" Chef threatens, TumTum backing away, both hands up placatingly.

"Hey boy- whoa. Are you guys OK?" Lovely's soft voice is full of concern as she stares at the carnage in my room.

Thank fuck my dad and his cronies had enough forethought to make the clubhouse fucking huge, including all our rooms, because my room looks like a fucking bombsite. There are screws and metal parts all over the floor, bits of wood that at some stage will be the bed our kid will sleep in. I'm surrounded by plastic and a poofy cushion thing. We must look like shit because Lovely carefully steps into the room, pity shining in her dark eyes. Her mouth opens as if to say something, before closing. She does this a few more times before she plants her hands on her hips, a look of determination coming over her.

"OK, you have around an hour before Chewy returns, and if she's off doing what we think she's doing-"

"She is. My dad is home tomorrow, Chewy called him to let him know he's going to be a grandpa." I can't help the smile that takes over my face.

Lovely nods, her dark hair swaying. "In that case we need this taken care of. Chef, step away. Go get a drink or some fresh air. TumTum, hand me those instructions. You do the same. Meet me back here in 5 minutes and we'll get this crib built. Without arguing."

Both men get up and move toward the door, only grumbling a little. Well, OK, grumbling a lot, but Lovely is too fucking sweet to get pissed at, so instead they'll do as the nice lady says and come back in five.

"Without their angry vibes in here you can finish building your swing cradle," Lovely says, quickly scanning the instructions before piling up the screws.

"My what?"

"That thing you're building. It's a baby swing cradle." I must stare at her blankly because she lets out a sigh before pointing to the box, "The UFO seat thing that Juno sits in."

I stare at her, then the front of the box, realizing what I'm meant to be making was right there. On the box.

"Rhodie, did you even read the instructions?" Lovely's lips twitch in the corners. I just know she wants to laugh, but instead she just raises her brows at me.

"No," I grumble, "I've had a lot on my mind."

She pats my hand, then continues sorting through crib pieces, laying them out just so, before reading the instruction manual again. Again, she finds matching pieces and lays them out in a neat pile, and I watch her. When she first arrived she was beaten down, frightened of a world she had no idea about. But instead of cutting herself off, hiding away in the cabin next to mine and Chewy's, she's here. Bossing around men twice her size. She's out running the front desk of Devil's Big Tow, calling in debts. She's raising her little girl, helping with the other babies and kids. She's a good friend of all the Ol Ladies and I know, deep down I know, that my brother feels more for her than he thinks he should. I also know that he treats her like she's the woman we first met. Timid, shy, scared. But she's far from that. I don't know why I never saw it before, but Lovely has a quiet strength about her, quite the opposite to Marx, but equally impressive.

"Lovely?"

"Hmm?" She answers distractedly, still concentrating on her task.

"You'll make a great Ol Lady one day."

Her cheeks pinken and she shakes her head, "Oh no, I think of you all as brothers," a sly smile comes over her face, "although I'd be lying if I said I hadn't wondered what Fox and Nitro get up to in the bedroom,"

I choke on spit. Or air or anything else you can choke on and my body heaves with a coughing fit as Lovely giggles, rummaging around for the bits and pieces she needs.

"Lovely! Holy fuck! You almost killed me!" My voice comes out as a wheeze and she throws her head back and cackles.

Once she calms down she smiles at me softly. "Truly, you're all like family to me."

"Every one of us?" I ask, brow raised.

Her cheeks darken and I know I've got her so I beam at her.

"Oh shush you! Just get back to building your UFO seat," She huffs good naturedly, before spinning to the door when

37

TumTum and Chef enter. "Good! You're back, let's do this!"

In no time we have the crib fully set up, and the UFO seat rotating weirdly in the corner. I have no idea what age our kid will be, but I'm hoping it's too old to use the seat because it kinda creeps me out.

"OH LUCY! I'M HOOOOOOME!" a voice calls and I'd be lying if I didn't get straight up and run to the common room.

Just before I hit the end of the hall I slow down to a stride. I mean, I don't wanna look too desperate! Walking through the doors my eyes scan the room, searching for my woman. The one who fucking completes me.

Standing there, just inside the doorway, Moss Davies behind her, is Chewy. My fucking reason for being. In her arms a little girl, head full of dark curls with a goddamn gator stuffy clutched to her chest. She turns her little head, her green eyes meeting mine and right then, right there I know that she is the one. She's our daughter.

Chewy beams at me, holding eye contact as I make my way across the room to them. I gently run my hand over our daughter's curls before leaning down and taking my woman's lips in a chaste kiss. Moving my gaze to the girl in Chewy's arms, I give her a smile.

"Hi there, little one, I'm Rhodie." She stares up at me before giving me a small smile as we stare at each other, taking each other in.

"Hey guess what?" Chewy's excited voice breaks my gaze with the little one in her arms.

"What, babe?"

"Me and Moss are friends!"

Pops

Ah shit. My eyes are wet. I blink them a few times to clear them. Can't show too much emotion around these fuckers, it'll ruin my street cred. But shit, watching my baby girl walk in that door with another little baby girl in her arms? That right there is enough to bring a tear to the eye of the toughest bastard around. A heavy arm drapes across my shoulder before I shrug it off, Tav's chuckle letting me know which of my grandsons is beside me.

"She did good, Pops."

I clear my clogged throat. "She sure fucking did, Son."

It's not like it's on everybody's list to have a kid, and truth be told, I never thought Chewy would. I've known her limitations and struggles since she was a little girl and I just never thought that motherhood was in the cards for her, and that was fine. Not all women want to grow up to be mothers and shit. Some want a career or to spend their life doing what they want. Chewy, though, Chewy has always, on some level, wanted to be normal. And in her own way, she got it. She went out there and made friends, she has a man who would fucking die for her, and she gave me a grandchild. I mean, sure, so he's a gator? Still, she loves him with all her heart and is the best gator mom anyone could ask for. But watching her step through those doors with a little girl held to her chest, one that looks like she did as a child? All wild hair and wide eyed? Well, that did something to this crusty old man's heart.

I feel Gus and Jules step up alongside me and Tav, and I gaze across the room. I see the grin on Chewy's face, the awe in her man's eyes, and pride blooms in my chest. More than I usually feel for her. When she was little and struggling with wanting to be like the other girls I'd talk her through it. Tell her that other little girls are boring and will all grow up to be married to boring men and have boring children. I'd tell her she was meant for more, and she fucking proved me right.

"She's gonna need us," Jules says in a low voice. "She's gonna be feeling a fuck load of things and it'll be overwhelming."

"Oh, speaking from experience, Jules?" Tav teases.

Jules doesn't say a word, just hits him with his asshole look, which Tav throws right back, before grinning.

"On the upside," Gus starts, "At least Chewy is self aware and listens to advice," he says drily, shooting a look at his brother.

"Yeah, yeah," Jules says, dropping a kiss on Juno's head.

Tav and Gus shuffle a little and I feel a small, soft hand slip into mine. "Aw look at her, Sydney."

"I know baby," I press a kiss to Debs' hair, and we watch as Rhodie lifts the little girl out of Chewy's hold, placing her on his hip as Chewy hugs one of his arms to her, staring up at the little girl with curiosity rather than wonder.

"Fuck this, I ain't waiting any longer, come on, lets go meet the newest Tombs," I say, ready to make a move.

"Wouldn't she be a Paxton?"

"Nope. Baby girl will always be a Tombs. Same with Chomper and this one."

I make my way across the room, ignoring the sniggers and Debs backhand to the gut with that tutting noise she does. I got a new grandbaby to meet.

Chapter 5

Chewy

I stare up at Laney-May and give her a little smile. She doesn't seem to be too frightened by all the people, and she seems to have taken to Rhodie quickly, settling into his big tattooed arms as if she was meant to be there. Shifting my gaze to my Ol Man, I feel my lips pull up into a wide smile, watching him talk quietly to the little girl in his arms. I know that he hasn't really spent that much time one-on-one with the other kids, but I've watched his interactions with them in the past and he's good with them. Just like he's good with me. He's calm and he reads people well. He knows when I'm upset or veering into over-stimulated. He knows how to make the world better.

He angles his head down to look at me and I stare up into his green eyes, eyes the same colour as Laney-May's, and he grins. A big, wide smile, as he leans down to press a kiss to my forehead.

"You did good, baby, but don't think I won't tan your ass later on."

"Wait, what for?" My brows pull down. What did I do this time?

"For going off on your own, risking your life to find this little girl."

I rear back, hands on my hips, "I didn't go off alone! I had Moss!" I spin to point at Moss who is backing toward the door, hands up, shaking his head.

"Don't bring me into this! I told you he wouldn't be happy,"

Rhodie glares in Moss's direction, before rolling his eyes, "Thank you for having her back, Moss."

He tips his head side to side. "Well, she did dangle a pretty fucking big carrot," he smirks.

Rhodie raises his brow, the sign he wants an explanation. Before I can open my mouth Marx comes stomping over.

"Chewy, looks like you found what you were looking for," he peers at Rhodie's - I mean, our daughter, his beard pulling up in the corners. I think he might be smiling, but it's hard to tell because I can't see his teeth.

He reaches his thick finger out and gently touches Laney's hand. I would call her by her full name but it's quite wordy. I wonder if Rhodie wants to give her a new name? I look back at Laney and decide that no, that's a terrible idea. Unless it's not quite her real name. Maybe I should look into that? I'm about to wander off when I remember that I'm meant to be a mom now, and I guess I can't just wander off. That's going to make things a little tricky, but I'm sure with a good routine and schedule I'll be able to make it work. Before I can arrange the next few hours in my mind my family comes striding toward me.

Shit. I forgot to tell them I was going to find Laney too. Whoops. As soon as Pops reaches me he pulls me into his arms and I snuggle in, wrapped up in the slightly talcum powdery smell of Pops. He also smells just a little spicy, which is whatever deodorant he wears, and it's a smell that is all Pops.

"You did good, kid." he whispers in my ear and I smile into his chest before he passes me over to Gus, who does the same thing.

Tav and Jules wait their turns, although Jules just wraps one arm around me and squeezes. He never has done full body hugs, well, other than with Violet and probably all those women he boned, but now that he has Juno he's retired that side of him.

He stares down at me and we share a look. I know he's trying to tell me that I can go to him if I need to decompress or ask about child related things, so I nod in understanding. Jules is perhaps the most like me, out of our siblings, so I know if I have an issue he'll be able to help. Violet walks up to him, giving him a kiss before kissing Juno on the cheek and turning to me, which then dislodges the memory that I have Candice Rogers in the van outside.

"Oh shiiiiii-rts." My gaze darts to Laney who doesn't look like she cares that I almost swore. "I forgot Candice! She's in the van. You're welcome, Violet!"

Vi's brows hit her hairline and Nat lets out a snort. "What a lovely present Chewy brought you, Vi."

Vi's look of shock fades until she grins at me. "So, what's the plan?"

"Whoa whoa whoa! Cool your jets ladies!" Marx says, holding his hands up, as if he could hold us back. "First off, we need to get as much information out of her as we can. Chewy," he turns toward me, "You've had a huge day, why don't you go settle in with your new little family and we'll take care of it for you."

"Huh?" I ask, confused. What the hell is he talking about? I'm the DRMC Icer. It's my job.

43

Well, actually, technically, it's Rhodie's job, but tomatoes, tomahtoes.

Marx steps a little closer, smiling softly down at me. "It's late Chewy, probably close to Laney-May's bedtime."

My eyes flick to the little girl and notice that yes, her eyes are starting to droop a little. She's snuggled into Rhodie's hold, and I can't imagine a better place to be.

"Oh yeah, good point. I never thought of that." I shrug. "But, me and the girls get to work Candice over. The DRMC men don't hurt women. But there's nothing in the bylaws that the Ol Ladies can't."

"Oh hells yeah!" Blanche whispers under her breath. Tav curses under his.

"Oh yes yes yes!" Mira hops up and down, clapping in time with her "yeses". "Oh this is gonna be sooooo good!"

"Babe, you are not going in there," Tank grumbles and then backtracks under his breath when Mira whirls on him.

Nat and Remy are already animatedly talking amongst themselves about something they saw on a true crime documentary while Vi's sisters, I have no idea why they're still here, are sitting with Ana and Lovely talking about who knows what, but apparently, they want in, too.

Marx lets out a long sigh, his giant hand scrubbing down his hairy face. "Is there any way you'll sit this one out?"

"No!" is replied by pretty much every woman in here.

Marx curses under his breath, before sharing a look with his brother, my Ol Man. "Chef, put our guest on ice. Chewy and the girls will visit her when they're ready,"

I grin and give my Girl Gang a thumbs up. "Rendezvous here tomorrow at 4?"

"It's a date!"

I grin and wave and throw thumbs ups over my shoulder as Rhodie shakes his head, leading me to our room and chuckling under his breath.

"Laney-May, your new momma is trouble."

I can't help but grin. Because yes, yes I am.

Rhodie

I lead my girls down the hall as if it's the most natural thing in the world. I have no idea how the fuck my life came to this. I mean almost two years ago I was living my life, enforcing and fucking like my life depended on it. Now I have a woman I'd do anything for, and I mean *anything* if what happened at Christmas is any indication, and a kid. A kid that we knew nothing about until an Ex-Bratva freaky dude with visions told us that we had a kid out there. You couldn't make this shit up.

Shaking the thoughts away I lead Chewy into our room, complete with a crib that Lovely assures me turns into a toddler bed when she outgrows it, and that weird ass UFO seat thing.

"Holy crap this looks great!" Chewy says, wide eyed. Then, as per Chewy she moves the crib just a little so it's sitting more square in the room. "Oh wow! And a little rocking seat for Chomper!" She claps her hands and looks at me with a huge smile. So of course I smile and nod. I'm not a total asshole.

We stare at each other a moment, holding eye contact before Chewy's gaze flits off, as usual. "So, what do we do now?" she whispers.

I freeze, because I was hoping she would know. "Ahhhhhh-"

"Knock knock," Mama Debs calls gently from the hall before walking in, "I know this is your first night as a *whanau* - family, but thought I'd offer a hand just in ca-"

"Yes!" I call, almost desperately, "I mean, please, we just realized we're not too sure what comes next."

Mama Debs looks between me, Chewy and Laney-May, a gentle smile on her face. "Well, let's see about getting the little one into the tub, a nice warm bath is always relaxing and it helps them settle down for sleep. Shall we start there?"

Chewy nods emphatically, and then watches intently as Mama Debs fills the bath, showing Chewy and me how to check the temperature and all that stuff. Undressing Laney felt a little weird. I mean, we've only just met, but Chewy had the idea to ask Laney if what we were doing was OK, and let her know that she was safe. I was so fucking proud of my woman, coming up with that solution that made us all a little more comfortable. The pride did a good job of tamping down the rage I felt that at no time did Laney complain. From what Chewy murmured to me of how she was found, I think Laney is used to lots of carers stripping her down for baths and what not. Well, that's going to fucking stop right here, right now. From now on the only people bathing my kid will be me and Chewy, and Mama Debs on occasion if she and Pops are babysitting.

By the time the bath was done and Chewy and I had gotten Laney dried, moisturized and dressed the little girl was almost asleep. We stood over her little bed for far too long, watching her eyes slowly blinking, until her dark lashes rested on her chubby cheeks and her breath evened out.

"You did good, you two. You're going to be the best parents little Laney could ever ask for," Mama Debs whispered before laying a warm hand on my cheek, then Chewy's. "Good night,

I'll see you for breakfast in the morning. We'll show the little one just how big a family she has now."

The door closes gently behind Debs and I lead my woman back into the bathroom, running the shower. Not saying a word I undress her, inch by inch her smooth skin comes into view, more beautiful than ever. Making sure the shower has heated up nicely I shuck my clothing, kicking my boots into the corner, before leading my woman into the hot water. I let the water pound down over her curls, then turn her back to me. Picking up her shampoo, I pour some into my palm, lathering it a little before massaging it into her thick, dark hair.

She lets out a little groan, and I ignore my hard cock nestled between her ass cheeks as I continue working the shampoo through her lengths.

"So, you're not mad?" Chewy's voice says around a moan as I dig my fingers in a little harder.

"Oh I'm pissed." She tries to whirl around but I firmly turn her to face the wall. "Not at you. Well, maybe a little at you. But mainly them. Happy Values, Candice Fucking Rogers. That little girl out there would let us do anything we wanted to her. She has no sense of fear or wariness."

Chewy nods in agreement. "Yeah. I researched it on the drive back. Any stranger anxiety she may have had would start to lessen at this age, however she seems more willing to attach herself to strangers than is normal," Chewy murmurs.

I finish my ministrations and let her rinse her hair before reaching for the conditioner and starting again.

"What do you think we should do about it?" I whisper, not wanting to wake Laney with our loud voices.

"Well, once you rinse the conditioner I'm going to suck your fat cock and swallow your cum. Then tomorrow I'm going to

47

learn all I can about looking after a toddler, and then I'm going to maim a bitch until I feel better about things."

A smile curls my lips as I rinse the conditioner out as quickly as I can. "Fuck I love it when you talk dirty to me."

Chewy grins up at me before sinking to her knees, licking her lips. Without using her hands she licks me from balls to tip, then back down, then up once more before engulfing my cock in her mouth. Her whiskey colored eyes gaze up at me, my length and width stretching her lips obscenely. I tuck a strand of wet hair behind her ear, then gently cup her face as my hips rock, sliding my length in and out of her hot little mouth.

Before long I'm fucking her with wild abandon, pumping my hips as she gags and spits on my cock like the dirty girl she is and I fucking love it. I can feel the tingle in the base of my spine, but I'm not going to cum down her throat, not tonight. Tonight I'm going to pound into her tight pussy, fucking out my frustrations until we're both sated and calm.

Pulling my hips back so my cock leaves the tight suction of her mouth with a little pop, I lift her by the underarms until she's standing. Turning her to the wall I drop to my knees, spread those plump cheeks and bury my tongue into her tight little asshole. We groan in unison as I keep tonguing her, my thick fingers parting her lips and running my finger from her wet hole to her clit, giving it a little pinch before travelling back the other way.

As usual my woman is dripping for me, and I can't help but drink up some of her juices before standing, spreading her cheeks with one hand, and grabbing and slapping my cock against her pussy a couple of times. A gentleman always knocks! Rubbing the crown of my dick through her folds, I let it bump her clit once, twice, before angling back and pressing into her waiting core. In one rough thrust I'm balls deep and I know I'm not going to last. Although judging by Chewy's whimpering and the way her pussy is spasming around my length, I don't think she is either.

"Please, Rhodie, please fuck me," Chewy murmurs quietly, bucking her hips back and forth, essentially fucking me.

"That's it baby, fuck me just like that. I want you to cum on my cock, then I'm going to fuck you until you can't remember your name."

She does exactly what I said, twerking all over me, fucking me, her hips working over my length until she explodes, biting into the meaty part of her hand to contain her wails so as not to wake anyone.

"Thats it, right there, fuck!" I growl, gripping her hips roughly as I pull her on and off my cock, my balls slapping rhymically as she bucks and grinds until her legs start to shake.

Fuck, mine feel weak too as I shoot load after load into my woman, painting her insides with my cum. I wrap my arms around her, pulling her back into me while we catch our breath.

"We are nailing this shit. We have a kid AND we just fucked," Chewy grins holding her hand up for a high five.

"Fuck yeah we are." I drop a kiss to her temple and then set about washing her all over again.

"Hey! We should have a team name. Or a family name or whatever."

"OK babe, what do you suggest?"

"Well, some families join their names together." Her face scrunches and I drop a kiss to her nose. "What about Team Ruesday? No, that's shit. Rewy? Ohh, what about Chodie?"

I freeze, surely she knows what a chode is, right?

"Yeah, I like that. Chodie has a good ring to it." She seems

49

so pleased with herself and I just don't have it in me to ruin it for her just yet. But I will. I refuse to have my family known as Team Chodie.

We finish up and dry off, and where we would usually sleep naked we both pull on underwear. Well I pull on my boxers, and Chewy pulls on my boxers and one of my tees. We gaze down at the little girl, fast asleep in the crib her family bought and built for her and we just....watch her.

"How long do you think is too long to watch someone sleep?" Chewy whispers, eyes on the little girl.

"Um, I'm not sure. Is it creepy that we're still doing it?"

"Maybe? I mean, I stare all the time, so maybe I can do it for longer than you," she shrugs.

"Hmm. Two more minutes then we go to bed." I pull Chewy into my arms, and we spend the next two minutes with our thoughts and our eyes on our newest family member.

Oh OK, maybe it was ten minutes.

Chapter 6

Chewy

I chew on my pancakes as I watch Laney sitting on the floor with Chomper. Rhodie put a muzzle on him to keep Laney safe and he's small enough to not knock her over or anything. Not that she would mind. She squealed and babbled a bunch of words as soon as she saw him, wriggling to get down out of Rhodie's arms.

"Chewy, we're meeting up at the diner for lunch today, it's kinda like our own DRMC mom's group. Wanna join?" Nat asks, her chunky daughter Rosie on her hip.

I tilt my head, looking in her direction. "I didn't know you had a mom's group."

"Well, it's not really. It's a get-together-for-lunch-and-spend-most-of-our-time-talking-about- our-kids group." Blanche answers, rubbing her big, swollen belly. I eye it for a moment because there's no way it can get bigger. Surely.

"OK. It makes sense that I wouldn't have been interested before. I mean, kids don't really interest me. Apart from mine, now that I have one. She seems quite smart too," I dart my gaze to see what she's doing. She's sitting babbling to Chomper, staring intently at his scales. One chubby finger gently touches one of his thicker scales as she pats him gently. Rhodie is sitting next to her, murmuring something, and she nods her head. She's learning. "Also, I'm sure I'll be able to get lots of information and pointers seeing as Blanche and Remy have old kids."

"Thanks," Remy says, but not in a thankful way. More of a sarcastic way.

"So, what time is lunch?" I ask, glancing back at Rhodie and Laney.

"We like to get there at 11.30, get the good seats before the lunch rush," Mira says with a huge smile.

My brows pinch in, Mira doesn't have children so I point out the obvious.

"Pshh," Mira flaps a hand at me, "I may not have kids, but I like the research. Might need it for a book one day."

"Fair enough," I shrug.

"Morning girlies," Pops greets everyone, dropping a kiss to the top of my head. "So, we meeting same time, same place?"

Tilting my head I stare at Pops for a moment, "Wait, you go to lunch with the Girl Gang too?"

"Of course I do." Pops gives me a funny look.

"I thought it was a Mommie's group?" I frown.

"When you lost your parents I became your mommy and your daddy as well as your Pops. Realistically I should have three groups with whom to share my knowledge, yet alas, I only have the one," Pops laments.

"I'm sure one is more than enough," Ana says under her breath as she walks over to drop a kiss on Pops' cheek.

She plops down next to Pops and hands JR over to him before

turning and greeting Laney with a big smile and a wave. Laney looks toward her and waves for a second, her attention back on Chomper's toenails.

"Gus got Marx business?" Lovely asks.

"Gus and Roman business. Roman was pulling in when we were," Ana answers, taking the plate of scrambled eggs Mama Debs presents her with. "Thanks Mama."

"Welcome, baby."

"Welcome, baby," I echo. I say it once more, wondering if it's something I could pull off, now that I'm a mom and all. Turning to Laney, I echo the words once more. "Welcome, baby." She frowns at me so I figure that one is not for me.

"Testing it out?" Pops says, bumping his shoulder with mine.

"Not for me," I sigh.

"Hey, it ain't for everyone," he says.

"I agree," Vi chimes in, Juno on her hip. "I couldn't pull it off either."

"I think the only person who could is Lovely," Remy joins in.

Nat, Mira and Blanche all nod while Lovely turns a little pink in the cheeks. "Welcome, baby," she says perfectly and it just fits. We all grin at her as she snuggles Bee and whispers it into her dark hair.

I like this. This weird lady bonding. Well, lady and Pops bonding. I mean, they're my girl gang anyway, but being a Mommy Girl Gang is different. It's new and kinda exciting. Standing abruptly, they all look toward me.

"I'm going to spend time with my daughter so I will have questions and ideas at lunch. I'll see you all then. Oh, and Ana? Ask Gus what his meeting was about. I may need to know the details."

Her brows furrow. "He usually briefs you after every meeting with Marx anyway."

"Yes but I'm on maternity leave for obvious reasons," I wave toward Rhodie and Laney, "so I will be multitasking home and work life. Having you brief me at lunch consolidates two things into one meaning I have more time to practice caring for Laney. I'm a little slow to do things at the moment, but Jules said that it's a good idea to try shaving off a second here or there every day. It's all practice, you know?" I tilt my head and glance at the Girl Gang.

"Yeah, we know what you mean," Ana says, and I ignore the twitches of the Girl Gang's lips. I'm sure if they thought about it deep enough they'll see that I am correct.

Leaving them to it I make my way to the rug where my little family sits, Chomper at the center, soaking up all the attention.

"Babe, did you know baby girl ate all her scrambled eggs?" Rhodie says, and I'm sure that's a look of pride on his face. Sometimes he looks at me like that and it makes my chest hurt in a good way.

"Good work, Laney!" I say, with enthusiasm because children like that kind of thing. Also, I've heard Vi's sister Jazz speak like that to the MC kids and she's a teacher so she should know the best way to get their attention and teach them things.

Laney gives me a smile and a clap and I can't help but grin back. The same smile stays on my face as I share a look with Rhodie, because clearly the child we have chosen is very clever. I can see how easy it is for parents to brag about their children. Although many parents have mediocre children. I'll need to research how to make sure Laney advances at the right stage for her age, or maybe even beyond.

"Babe? You've got that look on your face, maybe park that idea for a moment, yeah?" Rhodie says in his rough voice, like he's been gargling rocks his whole life.

"What idea?" I ask, avoiding eye contact.

"Not sure, but I can read you like a book and that look is a 'fall down the rabbit hole' look. Remember we decided we'd spend as much time having Laney get to know us as possible over the next few days."

"Yes, yes, trust me, I can multitask. I got this." I wave him off and move to stand.

Laney tilts her head back and moves to stand with me, gator stuffy held tight in her left hand as she reaches up for my hand with her right.

"Come on, Laney-May, it's reading time. Reading for good brain development should be done in little short bursts at your age, for optimum language absorption."

Rhodie snorts, picks up Chomper and waves a hand. "Lead the way, Professor Chewy."

Rhodie

"What is this music?" Cove whines in her overly loud voice.

"It sounds like an invasion!" Jovie adds in, messing around with a huge dinosaur Rider gave her.

Chewy ignores the question, instead concentrating on reading some type of chapter book to Laney, who is nestled in a beanbag. I doubt if she even knows what the hell Chewy is talking about, but she's quietly listening, her chubby fingers playing with her stuffy's feet. Her little fat foot is slowly moving back and forth over Chomper's tail as he snoozes.

"It sounds bad. SO bad. Why are we listening to this and not Metallica?" Cove asks.

"Because Metallica isn't good for brain development. Baroque music is," Chewy says, before turning the page and reading on.

"Metallica is good for dancing. This isn't good for dancing." To illustrate Cove raises her rock on horns and bangs her head in some type of frantic movement to match the beat.

If I'm being honest, it looks pretty identical to how I've seen her dance to rock, but what would I know? Jovie giggles and gets up to copy Cove while Elio sits ramrod straight next to Laney's bean bag listening to Chewy. His brain is probably soaking up all the classical music and shit. As if the kid needs to be any smarter.

A heavy hand lands on my shoulder and I turn in the tiny fucking kid chair Chewy made me sit in to see my dad smiling down at me. Grinning, I jump up and throw my arms around my dad, giving him heavy thumps on the back to match his on mine.

"Fucking good to see you, old man!"

"Yeah yeah, smartass. Now, is that one my grandbaby?" Mad Dog's eyes are laser focused on Laney, a look of awe on his face. "Fuck, you couldn't get a kid that looked more like you and Chewy if you birthed her yourself. Holy shit, Rhodie!"

I nod in agreement, because he's right. Laney is the perfect mix of me and Chewy. Her head is full of wild, dark curls, she has tanned skin and big green eyes, identical in color to mine. At this point we have no idea what her personality will be like or how much what she's been through will affect her in her life, but it doesn't matter. She's ours, through thick and thin, good and bad. I mean, shit, it's not like me and Chewy are perfect. We fucking kill people for a living. A frown pinches my brow before

I remember what Chewy tells me all the time when I sink into the darkness.

"We do what we do, to keep others safe. We protect them from the bad and we give them their lives back. With our actions they get closure. Rhodie, you are a good person that does bad things to make the world a better place. That's one of the things I love about you. The other is your big cock."

I huff out a laugh as I shake off the memory.

"All good, Son? Lost ya there for a bit." Dad's green eyes, just like mine and Marx's assess me, looking for what, I don't know.

"Yeah, just had a moment."

"You went dark, huh?"

I nod, eyes still on my family.

Mad Dog lets out a sigh, "If you need a session Son, just let me know." I nod at him, "Good, now introduce me, shit, how long does an old man have to wait to meet his granddaughter?"

I roll my eyes and huff out a laugh. "Come on then."

We walk past Cove and Jovie who are still acting like they're in a mosh pit and dad raises his brows.

"The dark haired girl and boy belong to Chewy's brother Tav. The other one is Wire's."

"Shit, you lot have kids coming out the wazoo," Dad chuckles.

"Ain't that the truth," I answer before turning to Chewy. "Babe," I call, pulling her out of her reading.

Her head snaps in our direction, her eyes growing huge when her gaze lands on Mad Dog.

"Mad Dog! You're home!" She jumps up and instead of throwing herself into his arms immediately, she bounces on the balls of her feet, flapping a little, unsure what to do.

Mad Dog opens his arms and she bustles into them, gently tapping her hands on his back before pulling back.

"You're back just in time! Laney and I have just finished up our chapter for this morning."

She drops to her knees in front of Laney, looking into the toddler's face, "Laney, this is your grandfather-" her brows pinch and she looks back at us, "What do we call you? Laney already has a Pops. What do you want to be called, Mad Dog?" she asks my dad.

Mad Dog thinks, his mouth in a straight line, brows furrowed. "Well -"

"Doggy," A tiny voice says quietly.

My head snaps toward Laney, cuddling her gator, her finger pointing in Mad Dog's direction. I crouch down next to Chewy, in front of our daughter.

"That's right baby. That's Mad Dog," I grin at her.

"Doggy!" she says, stronger now as her feet kick.

"Well, there you go," Dad booms. "Looks like I'm gonna be known as 'Doggy' to my grandkids," he throws his head back and laughs, then grips my shoulder and shoves me out of the way, making Laney giggle.

He holds his hands out to her and she practically throws herself into his hold. His grin is fucking infectious and I watch him murmuring to Laney, rocking her this way and that.

"Shit, what the fuck!" Mad Dog stumbles back, eyes wide, gripping Laney to his chest. "What in the fuck!? That's a fucking gator!" He's gaping down at Chomper who decides at this very moment to lazily open his mouth and try and have a go at Dad's boot.

"Oh, this is your very first grandchild! Meet Chomper!" Chewy says, scooping up our gator baby and holding him up to my father who stumbles back.

He's fucking speechless and I'd take my phone out to record

this if I knew I would stay alive long enough to show it to all the brothers.

"Chewy, why, how the fuck- shit you know what? I don't want to know." He loosens his grip on Laney, rubbing one hand down his face. "I'm sure he's a lovely little gator but let's just agree that he stays far away from Doggy, OK?"

I snort, he's not gonna live this down. He became a grandfather and now he's referring to himself in the third person.

"It's OK, baby. Doggy loves you, just not up close," Chewy murmurs, running her hands down Chomper's back.

"Aunt Chewy! Can Chomper dance with us?" Jovie asks, looking all damp from the amount of bouncing her and Cove have been doing.

Elio who was sitting listening to Chewy read has obviously had enough of what's going on because he's now taken the chapter book and moved into a quiet corner, reading to himself.

"He's not good at dancing, but I'm sure he'll try," Chewy says, putting Chomper on the floor in the middle of the two girls who dance around him like women dance around their handbags in clubs.

"Hey babyg-," Pops' words cut off as he freezes in the doorway, taking in Laney in Mad Dog's arms. "What the fuck?" he murmurs, eyes narrowing at the scene.

"Sid! Good to see you again," Dad offers his hand then pulls it back when all Pops does is stare at it. "So, how about this little miracle huh? We're now grandpa's in-law," Dad grins at Laney then back at Pops, his eyes still narrowed.

"Yes, isn't that something," Pops answers. He holds his hands out to Laney, a big smile on his face, "Wanna come give Pops a little cuddle?"

She grins at Pops then points to my dad, poking him in the

59

chest. "Doggy!"

Pops' hands spring back, like he's been burned, shock on his face.

"Doggy!"

"Yeah, sweetheart," Pops swallows and clears his throat, "yeah, that's Mad Dog." Laney grins and leans her head on Dad's shoulder.

He stares for a moment longer, eyes getting narrower and narrower the longer he stares at my father.

"You OK there Sid?" Dad asks, looking concerned.

"Oh yeah, just...thinking." He leans around Mad Dog and Laney. "Elio, mind giving me a hand with...something?" His eyes dart to Dad, then back to Elio who carefully places a bookmark into the book he was reading, and places the book back on the shelf, before coming toward us.

"Explosions?" he asks, looking up at Pops, ignoring everyone else in the room.

Pops' eyes flick to Mad Dog, then back, "No, not just yet. Let's go brainstorm." He turns stiffly, then throws a wave over his shoulder, bustling out, Elio hot on his heels.

We watch him leave and then Dad turns to me, "Son, I know I've been away for a while but holy shit, this place is chaos."

I throw my head back and laugh, he has no fucking idea.

Chapter 7

Chewy

I'm feeling triumphant and have decided that mine and Rhodie's child really is superior to other children. Thanks to the routine I have implemented Laney managed to do her reading, have structured play time, spend time with family and friends, a short brain break with a power nap and now I have successfully unfolded her pushchair from the back of the SUV and strapped her into it. I timed it so I arrived at Girl Gang Moms group exactly on time, but I can see walking through the doors that not everyone is here yet.

"Over here Chewy!" Mira waves enthusiastically.

To begin with I was unsure about Mira. She is very bubbly and warm and not really into murder in real life, however I got to know her and I appreciated the warmth she brings. Each of the Girl Gang brings new skills to share with the group and I feel that's a good thing. Glancing at Lovely, I note how much she has changed since being a Girl Gang member. Our skills are rubbing off on her and vice versa. It's a good thing.

"Sorry I'm late! Jr slept late," Ana says, rushing in with her designer buggy and her silky blouse. She is very fancy. And not good at keeping a sleep schedule, obviously. "So, who are we waiting on?"

"No one, we're all here. Kaia, the new owner, will be bringing us a selection of new muffins to try," Remy says, excitedly.

I look forward to meeting this Kaia woman. I'm not sure what all happened but when we were surveilling this place Judge and her had some type of interaction that made the brother even quieter than usual. And he refuses to come here.

"Ladies, I have been usurped," Pops sighs dramatically after his big announcement.

There are gasps and giggles around the table before Remy asks, in a concerned voice, "By who?"

"Mad Dog," he grumbles under his breath.

"Huh?" Nat asks.

"Mad Dog. Rhodie's father. My darling granddaughter has ditched me." His shoulders slump as he fiddles with a napkin, tearing it to pieces.

"Sage?" Blanche asks.

"No, not that sweet baby girl. She's a good girl. All she does is study and look after her old Pops."

I side eye Pops. More often than not Sage is mooning over Takoda, Chef as he's now called. It's not subtle if even *I* can pick up on it.

"Cove then?" Ana asks, trying to hide her smile.

"Or Bee or Rosie?"

"No, not those sweet babies either." His eyes dart toward me and Laney. "It's Chewy's kid that has forsaken me."

Looking around the table I can see everyone trying hard not to laugh at him. He can be ridiculous at times.

"Anyway I need help. I can't have Mad Dog swanning in,

taking my grandbabies."

"You have like, a ton of them. You've claimed them all," Nat says, jiggling Rosie in her lap. To prove her right Pops leans over and squishes Rosie's fat thigh, saying something or other to her in baby talk.

He should really stop doing that. Evidence suggests that talking in normal, adult language is perfectly fine for children and babies.

"I'm going to accelerate Laney's learning," I blurt out.

"Ooooookay. And what does that entail?" Lovely asks.

It's a good question. From what I know education for girls wasn't a huge priority at The Keep where she grew up.

"Well, I have her on a learning schedule. For 20 minutes every morning and evening I will read language-enhancing literature to her whilst playing classical music to stimulate her brain waves. Once she's older we will add in math and perhaps even a second language. I may need your help with that Vi, seeing as you speak Spanish."

She stares wide-eyed at me while Juno gives me RBF. It really is uncanny.

"That sounds like a, um, intense plan, Chewy. But I'm sure it will be beneficial," Lovely says, almost too politely.

"Well, now that's been stated, how am I going to usurp Mad Dog?" Pops asks.

The table starts brainstorming, but none of it sounds very good. Especially Mira's idea which was to maybe share Laney. By the horrified look on Pops' face, he's not down for that.

"Here you are ladies, and man," a short, curvy brunette angles herself between Blanche and Remy, to place a large platter of muffins down in front of us.

"Ohhhh they look so good!" Mira claps and bounces in her

seat, the rest of us agreeing with her.

They do look delicious, and I want to take one, but I have questions. "So, a little while back we had a, ah, special operation here in your diner."

She smiles warmly and bobs her head. "Oh yeah, I had Chef and TumTum in the kitchen. They're so funny."

"Ah, yeah, I guess. Anyway, There was an exchange between you and one of our DRMC members, Judge?" Her brows pull down a little. "So I just wanted to know what that was about."

"Chewy!" Ana hisses, but I ignore her. I want to get to the bottom of this, and Judge will never tell me.

"Judge?" She snorts, "When I knew him he was Leo. We were best friends. Then he became the small town quarterback and turned into a popular meathead asshole. He may have changed for the better, but I'm not holding my breath to find out." She turns stiffly, taking a few steps before turning back to look at us, a tight smile on her face. "I hope you enjoy the muffins."

"Well, it sounds like Judge has been a naughty boy," Blanche grins.

Before we can gossip about what exactly happened there, Jr starts making a fuss until his mother feeds him a small piece of muffin. I know Laney can handle most foods, so I select one of the delicious morsels and break a little piece off, holding it up to her mouth, mimicking Nat and Ana. Laney gobbles it up, then spits it down her front.

"Hey! What was that for?" I ask her.

I pick up a piece in my other hand, not the one that went near Laney's mouth, and I pop it in mine. The flavours burst on my tongue and I try not to moan in appreciation. That doesn't stop the rest of the table,

"Holy fuck, I don't care what Judge did, he needs to marry

64

that woman so we can get unlimited muffins." Pops' eyes pop open. "Do NOT tell my Ol Lady that!"

We all snicker, and I try Laney on another piece. She does the same thing, this time spitting it over herself and me. "What the hell are you doing? Nothing I've read said this happens," I mutter.

"Chewy, I know you love research, but maybe this is less research and more scientific observation?" Lovely offers, Remy nodding in agreement.

"Huh. Like David Attenborough learning the movements of a particular species. Instead of a new species, it's my daughter. Interesting." I stroke my pretend moustache. I never once thought to do that, but I will from now on. A two pronged research attempt could be perfect for me. "In this case I think the research is telling me that she is not fond of chocolate muffins."

"You think?" Blanche says, taking the chocolate muffin off Laney's plate and placing it on hers.

"Violet, fancy seeing you here, with these, um," the owner of the voice looks over our table, "friends?"

"Yes Josh, they are my friends, and guess what? They don't care where my mother is from." Violet says, throwing her half-eaten muffin onto her plate and staring him down.

"Wait, *this* is Josh? This-" Blanche waves her hand in the air, indicating the boring looking man in front of us. "This is him? The one that was mean to your Mom and then dumped you?" Blanche shoves the rest of her muffin into her mouth and struggles to get her pregnant bulk out of her chair to stand next to Vi.

"This is him?" Mira asks, her voice almost a screech.

"I've never seen a human embodiment of a ham sandwich,"

65

Pops says.

We all stare as he gapes. "No, come on Vi. We were perfect together, you just needed a little.... refining."

"Oh hell no!" Nat throws down her napkin and stands, as do the rest of the Girl Gang.

Oh, it's so on.

Rhodie

"So brother, you wanna tell me what the hell is going on with you?" I raise a brow at Judge and stare him down. I'm not letting him get away without answering.

Which is why I made him go for a ride with me. I figure a little wind therapy is what he needs to get his head in order.

"Leave it in the past, brother."

"Like you clearly haven't?" I goad.

He huffs out a long sigh before turning to look at me. We're both parked up next to Rose Grove's town square, eating hot dogs from a street van because Judge refuses to go into the diner. "You ever do something when you were younger that truly fucked up one of your best relationships?"

I chew my mouthful, staring at him. "You talking bout cheating on a girl?"

"Yes. No. Fuck, I don't know!"

Both my brows raise of their own accord. Judge never struck me as the type of guy to play around like that, but I guess we were all young and dumb once.

"What do you mean, you don't know? Fairly certain it's easy

to know if you're cheating on a girl."

Judge scrubs a hand over his bald head, and then down his face. "Look, I had a best girl friend, inseparable since we were kids. We fooled around a couple of times, lost our virginity to each other, that kind of shit. But we were never dating or going steady or anything. Anyway, the last time I saw her, she'd come to talk to me, said it was important."

"And?"

"I was with my new friends, I'd made quarterback and suddenly found myself popular, that sort of shit. She kinda caught me getting a blow job from a girl," he cringes and I fucking feel for him.

"But you guys were never anything official? Not dating?"

He shakes his head, a wistful look on his face. "No. By the time she came around to talk we hadn't done anything for like a month or so. We only slept together twice and went about our normal lives."

"Well, it definitely wasn't cheating. That little lady in the diner, was it her? Did she think you were cheating on her?"

He lets out a soft growl. "Yeah, it's her. But-" he looks away, a frown marring his features, "I don't think it was the blowjob, as such. Argh, fuck this is embarrassing and makes me look like an asshole," he shakes himself off. "So, I was off my face, hanging with the jocks and the cheerleaders and she turned up asking to speak to me. My dick was in Chelsea Master's mouth and some of the jock kids started calling her names, Geek Girl, Dweeb, that sorta shit. Fuck, at the same time Chelsea tickled my balls and I giggled. That one giggle broke her fucking heart man. I could see it on her face. It was one thing to be getting a blowjob, but she always had a rough time making friends and me, her fucking best friend laughs at her with all these jock losers?" He looks toward the diner, face screwed up. "The look on her face, fuck, it screws my guts up thinking about it."

I close my eyes and fuck, my heart goes out to the brother. I mean, yeah, it was a shitty thing to do, but hell, we all do dumb shit when we're in high school. We're young, dumb and really fucking full of cum.

"Did you apologize at least?"

"I hid away for two days, trying to come up with a big fucking gesture. I turned up at her place, flowers, chocolates, her favourite DVD's, the fucking lot all to find her and her father had moved. No idea where they went."

"And now she's back."

"And now she's back and full of piss and vinegar and I can't even blame her."

I slap a hand on his shoulder and give him a shake. He'll figure it out. Shit if he ever wants to eat at the diner again, he'll have to. Vibrating in my pocket has my thoughts changing direction. Glancing at the screen I see Moss's name flashing.

"Moss? Don't tell me my Ol Lady needs your assistance again."

"Not if you get there first. Got a call from the diner, Chewy and her gang of merry ladies have kicked off on some poor schmuck."

"Ah, shit, is it bad?"

"Fucking hope so. He's Vi's ex boyfriend and he's an absolute douche lord. You take this one, and I'll come down if it escalates." He hangs up at the same time I hang my head.

"What's wrong?" Judge asks and I know I'm going to have to drag him to the diner with me. With the number of Ol Ladies we have, this is going to take more than me to calm the situation down.

"Got a scene at the diner, need your help, brother."

His dark eyes bore into mine and he blows out a breath before he nods. "Let's go."

We throw our legs over our bikes and leave them where we parked. The diner is just across from where we were sitting, so we jog across the road. I'm about to push through the door when I freeze at the scene inside. The patrons that aren't attached to the MC are all staring wide-eyed. One random old lady is holding Jr, while another is holding Rosie. Bee is kicking her legs in her car seat, where she is sitting next to Juno in hers atop a table with teenage girls eating fries. Laney is strapped into her stroller, her legs kicking, one fist in the air yelling an almost Xena like cry as she frowns at the scene in front of her. Some skinny, pasty guy is laid out across the table while all the women hold him down. No, scrap that. Pops, Lovely, Remy, Ana and Mira are holding him down. Blanche, Nat and Chewy are covering the guy in hot sauce while Vi is yelling "How do you like that spice? Huh, *pendejo*?"

I can see a little smirk on Chewy's face as the dude squirms and whines, so she pops him in the middle of the forehead with a teaspoon. I try to hide my chuckle as I pull open the door and walk in, Judge at my back.

"What the fuck is going on?" I say out loud, hoping to draw the attention of the MC women. No such luck.

The short, dark-haired owner comes bustling over, completely ignoring Judge.

"Look, I'm sure this looks bad, but the patrons and I are in agreement. This dick needs to learn his lesson. You don't talk shit about anyone's mama," she nods her head decisively before turning to walk away.

She makes it two steps before she spins back around. "Maybe

69

leave them for a couple of minutes, I want to see what they do with the lime. Once they do that you can break them up." Her eyes flick to Judge, her cheeks pinken and she sucks in a breath looking nervous more than angry. Interesting.

"Ah shit," I mutter as the guy screams like a little girl.

"There's sauce in my eye! It burns!" he's winking frantically, I'm guessing to get the sauce out, but he's shit outta luck.

"Oh, I know what neutralises that," Chewy says in a sweet voice.

"Lime juice! Let me help you," Vi laughs maniacally as she gets ready to squirt lime juice into his eye.

I tuck my lip and let out an ear piercing whistle. Yes, it's not only Marx that can stop a room with a whistle.

"That's enough now ladies." The whole diner lets out a collective "aw" and starts bitching under their breath. "I'm sure he's learned his lesson."

"No, I don't think he has," the old woman holding Rosie says. "That guy is a Grade A asshole *and* racist,"

"Yup, I say lime juice to the eye," her old lady friend shouts, jiggling Jr. The diner lets out a cheer and shit, this guy must have really rubbed everyone up the wrong way.

Unfortunately, we don't need any heat coming back on the MC. We already skirt the law in one way or another. The last thing we need is to draw the attention of Rose Grove PD thanks to the antics of the women.

"Put. The. Lime. Down." I say in a firm voice. Oh OK, I growl, because I know these women are hard of hearing sometimes.

"Ugh, why do you have to come and shit all over our fun? Huh, Shitstain?" Pops growls. Then he eyes Laney before turning his gaze on me. He and I hold eye contact, knowing that as soon as one moves, the other will swoop in and snatch her up.

I lunge then pull back, faking him out. Due to his advanced age he falls for it, pulling back once he realizes, allowing me to get to Laney first, unbuckle her and cuddle her to me.

She throws her hands up and yells, gifting me a huge smile. "Hey, baby girl. You been cheering on Mama?" She grins and turns toward Chewy, pumping her little fist out and yelling at the wimpy ass motherfucker who is whimpering on the table top while Blanche whispers in his ear. "You're gonna be a little trouble maker like Mama, huh? Damn, Daddy will be busy." I may let out a sigh, but there's a little flutter in my stomach. I can't think of a better role model for a little girl than my woman.

The woman who has just squeezed the lime wedge, "accidentally" getting it in pasty guy's eye. Pasty guy starts squealing like a stuck pig and cheers break out amongst the diner patrons. Shaking my head at her I hold out my hand, my woman taking it without question. I pull her until she's plastered to the side of my body, exactly where she belongs. With my two girls in my arms I feel like the fucking king of the world.

"Well, not quite the outcome I would have expected, but a satisfying one nonetheless." Moss's voice says from over my shoulder.

"How long have you been lurking?"

He throws a smirk my way. "Since I called you. I was in an unmarked cruiser outside watching shit go down." His face breaks out into a grin.

"Officer! Officer! Are you going to do anything about this? This, this, it's assault! That's what it is!" Pasty guy yells, spittle flying from his mouth.

"I guess it is," Moss answers, nodding gravely but staying exactly where he stands, hands in pockets.

Pasty waves his arms wildly in the direction of the women,

71

who have gone back to eating their muffins, babies on their laps. Judge has joined them, chewing on what looks to be a blueberry muffin. He keeps glancing at the little diner-owner lady, but she's doing a fucking stellar job at ignoring him.

"So? Aren't you going to do anything?"

"You know what? I don't think I will. Let this be a lesson to you, don't diss anyone's mother ever again. Especially mine," Moss's voice drops to a fucking scary tone at the end there and Pasty must get the picture because he lets out an indignant huff before tucking tail and leaving the diner to the cheers of the old women and teenage girls that are in their booths.

"Well, now that's sorted. Wanna muffin?"

Chapter 8

Chewy

R hodie has me gently by the elbow as he leads me into the clubhouse with Laney on his hip. I'm sure he's worried I'm going to start some shit. Not that it was me that kicked things off at the diner. That was actually Vi and Blanche. I'm not too sure if I should feel irritated that he thinks I'm a troublemaker, or proud.

"What the fuck?" Rhodie comes to a complete stop, breaking my stride.

There, in the middle of the common room is Pops, and I think he's flexing. How the hell did he get here so fast when he was with us at the diner?

"What the hell are they doing?" Rhodie says out loud, to anyone who might answer.

"I can't be too sure, I've only been here for like 10 minutes," Switch booms, "but I think it's some type of flexing competition?"

"Is that all you got old man?" Pops taunts Mad Dog, who scowls and then doubles down.

I snuggle tighter into Rhodie, jiggling Laney's fat little foot. I've never seen such chubby toes, so I'm not sure if it's normal or not. Although judging by her chubby legs and all over stubby body, I'm sure it's fine. Turning back to the competition the old men have going, I watch as Pops pulls the Apollo pose, his left arm and hand flexing into a claw like hold, while his right is held out in front, like the statue of Apollo in classical art. Mad Dog pulls his own version, and I am impressed. Laney is too as she raises her arms and yells "Doggy" at the top of her lungs.

"Shit, Pops ain't gonna like that," Rhodie chuckles, and he's right.

"That's it! I'm pulling out the big guns!" Pops growls.

He hoists his chinos higher, the middle seam now cutting between the globes of his glutes. He bends a little forward, hands on his waistline before he flexes, his trousers almost devoured by his muscular buttocks.

"My eyes!" Switch yells as Fox and Nitro start taking bets from the brothers and Ol Ladies over who will be the winner.

Mad Dog's eyes narrow and he gets set to mimic Pops when Marx comes stomping down the hall. "What the fuck is going on in here?" He takes one look at Pops derriere on display and his face morphs from confusion to disgust. I know those looks.

"Sidney! Stop showing off what belongs to me!" Mama Debs says, bustling in and hiding Pops' ass with her tea towel.

"Thank you Mama Debs," Marx says with a nod. "Can you two please just agree to both be the best grandpa in the world?"

"No!" Pops yells. "No way! We're tied, I just need one more win!"

"What do you mean you're tied?" I ask. He's been with me most of the afternoon.

"This morning Sid challenged me to a game of darts. Then

74

foosball." Mad Dog says.

"They had a Lego-off as well, both built houses and I judged," Rider adds.

"I judged the coloring competition," Dex says, his hand raised.

Mad Dog and Pops both nod. "We're tied. And I'm sure I would have won the flex off if you lot hadn't interrupted," Pops grumbles.

"I know a way you can break your tie," Vi says, from her position leaning against Jules, Juno on her hip.

"What you got?" Mad Dog raises a chin in her direction.

"Well, my sister Jazz, you know she's an art teacher right? Well, she's been taking her kids out to draw in interesting places around town. They went to the park to draw trees, the diner to draw patrons, why don't they come here and draw you too?" Vi offers.

Pops and Mad Dog share a look. I'm pretty sure they're both confused. I am too.

"But that's not a competition," I say, "There is no clear winner." I tilt my head to the side.

"Well, seeing as they both like to pose, the winner will be whoever holds the pose longest," Vi grins.

"That sounds easy as shit," Pops scoffs.

"Well, we'll see, won't we?" Jules grins, kissing Vi on the top of her head.

Hmmm, I think there may be more to this posing than I once thought, especially with the way Jules and Vi are grinning and chuckling between themselves. Darting my eyes back to Pops and my grandfather-in-law, I watch as they share a look.

"Set it up," Pops says with a decisive nod.

"Great, now that we have that sorted and I'm going to have a class full of kids in my clubhouse that no one actually fucking ran by me, can we please talk about the bitch we have in the Rev Room?" Marx grumbles.

"Oh yeah, forgot about her in all the excitement," I say. I mean, it wasn't hard to forget about her. She is of no use to me anymore.

"Tell us what she knows," he nods.

"It's not much. She's the face of the whole set up. She's damn loaded, and all that through offshore accounts and shell corporations. But she's not the brains or the person who set that up. She works for some guy named Tito Caram -"

"What the fuck?" Sniper booms, stomping his way closer to where I'm standing.

My head tilts sideways as I take in his posture. He's breathing heavily, brows lowered, fists clenching at his sides. "Sniper, do you know Tito Caram?"

"On the streets he's known as 'Serpiente'," he grits out. "He's a known acquaintance of the Cordoza Cartel. Roman fucking said he'd handled them," Sniper growls, spinning to look at Marx.

I nod, Roman did say that. When the shit hit the fan with Blanche and Eden's Keep, Roman went in and cut the head off the Cordoza Cartel, taking out the leaders and leaving the seven-year-old son. Marx's jaw ticks with the revelation that perhaps not everyone was taken care of.

"Ana?"

Ana steps forward from where she had been standing leaning against the bar with Gus.

"On it, Marx," she raises a finger, cell phone to her ear already.

"Anything else I should know, Chewy?" Marx asks, brow raised.

"That's all she knows. Tito brought her on to act as the face of the company. Single older woman with fertility issues that can relate to the families that want to adopt? She's perfect. Slowly over time Tito 'promoted her' into running the baby farms and keeping the kids in another facility that she'd check on or lead tours for prospective parents. Said she knew it was wrong but the money was good. Oh, and she's not the only one. He has this same setup in states all along the I-10 corridor."

Marx pinches between his brows and takes a deep breath. I get it, the last thing we need is more trouble. "She got a way to contact this Tito?"

"Already cloned her phone. He's been sending non stop messages since after the raid the other night. Instructions telling her to ship the kids to the other locations and to clear out the accounts but he's been radio silent the past 3 and a half hours," I answer.

Marx runs a hand over his beard. "Do me a favor?" I nod at Marx. I'd do anything for him. He's my Pres. "Get rid of the bitch."

"Sir, yes sir!" I salute as he rolls his eyes. "Girl Gang?" All my girls stand, handing the babies over to their fathers or grandfathers. "Let's do this!"

Rhodie

"This feels weird as shit," Rider complains.

He's not wrong. We have a guest in the back shed, and yet all the MC men are sitting in the common room with kids running around. Prospect picked up the big kids half an hour ago, so Sage is busy changing all the babies one by one while the bigger little kids are fucking around with some contraption Elio is building.

"Here, Uncle Gus. Jr is all cleaned up and probably ready for his nap."

"Thanks Sweetheart," Gus replies, taking his son down the hall to the room we turned into a nursery. So far we have four cribs in there and a toddler bed for Laney. Finding out she wasn't a tiny baby helped me relax into my role. Little babies like Juno, Bee, Jr and Rosie scare me some.

Mad Dog drops down next to me on the couch, giving Laney's hand a squeeze. She smiles up at him and holds her hands out so I transfer her over to my dad's bulky arms.

"So, you wanna tell me what happened with Molly?" I ask, just as Marx takes a seat next to us.

"We grew apart, I guess. Wanted different things," he answers, snuggling Laney into him.

"What did you want that she didn't?" Marx asks in his rumbling voice.

"I wanted to be closer to you boys. The DRMC. You're starting to settle down, have families," Mad Dog jiggles Laney, to illustrate the point.

"Not me," Marx scoffs before jabbing a thumb in my direction. "Him."

Mad Dog hits Marx with his "don't give me that bullshit" look that he perfected years ago after having two boys try to pull the wool over his eyes. "You tryna tell me there's nothing going on with you and that dark-haired woman? Lovely, is that her name?"

Marx shuffles in his seat, turning his head to stare intently at the wall. "Nothing is going on."

"Really? Huh, I could have sworn something was going on," Mad Dog says, scratching at the stubble on his cheek.

"Look, she's a nice girl, alright? But that's all she is. She's too damn young and doesn't know anything about the fucking world," Marx growls, sitting up, challenging our father.

Mad Dog doesn't flinch, just stares Marx down. "Is that what she told you, or what you think? Because you know, a good Pres listens to his people. If talking isn't their strength he reads the situation til he has a bead on it."

"You think I don't know that? I'm the fucking Pres for a reason! You trusted me to lead, so I'm leading." Marx scowls, his fists balling.

"Yeah, you are, I'm not denying that, Son. What I'm saying is, you can't make decisions for your people without hearing them or seeing what they need. That woman doesn't need you coddling her. I think if you were honest with yourself you'd see that."

Marx runs a hand down his face, then places his hands on his knees, pushing up to stand. "Lovely is a brother's sister-in-law. Outside of that, she's none of my concern."

"Um, Rhodie? Chewy wants you," Lovely's sweet voice breaks the tension between Mad Dog and Marx and I see the moment Marx's shoulders slump.

"Lovely, I-"

Lovely holds her hand up, silencing Marx. "I got it, Pres." She nods then turns on her heel, walking through the kitchen, headed for the Rev Room.

Raising my brows at Mad Dog he shoos me away, "Go, I got Laney. Besides, it's nice to hold her without Sid giving me the death glare. Where is he anyway?"

"Don't you know? He's one of the founding members of the

Girl Gang," I laugh, headed for my woman. She calls, I come running.

Walking into the Rev Room I come to a complete stop. "What the fuck?" I whisper to myself. Instead of the usual blood and guts, there's two almost empty bottles of wine and Candice has had a makeover of sorts. It's not a good one, judging by how much of her hair is missing, and someone has given her some large, black eyebrows. Leaning closer I notice blood seeping from them. Holy shit! Did they tattoo them on?

"Oh hey Babe! You're just in time, we're about to give Candice here some lip filler," Chewy grins.

"I thought you were meant to be getting rid of her?"

"Well, yeah, but first we thought we'd have some fun. She likes plastic surgery so much, we figured we'd help her out. Besides, she may let slip some more secrets. Us Girl Gang can be quite persuasive," Chewy grins as Pops starts alcohol swabbing Candice's face.

"Shhhhh Tito saysh that I'm the bessht of all his women," Candice slurs.

Raising a brow at Chewy she shrugs, "The wine was for her. We're doing one of those Botox parties."

"We even have canapes!" Mira says excitedly. I do a double take when I see her here. She's not like Chewy or Blanche or Nat, or shit, even Vi. Mira is like Lovely and Remy and Ana. They're nice ladies who don't need to be involved in all this shit.

Before I can say anything to her Ana pipes up, "Get that look off your face, Rhodie. We're not weenies. We can handle this shit. Especially when this bitch was going to sell your daughter, our niece. That shit is personal."

"Amen, sister!" Mira says, with a hand in the air.

"OK, OK. So, what do you need me for?"

"Oh, we need you to hold her still. She's a slippery sausage," Chewy grins.

"Wait, I watched four of you hold down that pasty guy at the diner?" I look around at the faces, including Pops.

"Yeah, but she's stronger than that pussy," Vi answers.

"And to think you thought you loved him!" Blanche crows, then cackles, holding her large stomach.

"Shut it, you! I was confused!"

"It was more than that, girl," Nat joins in the teasing.

I blow out a breath and get on with it. These women talk at the speed of light when they all get together, and I can't keep up. I wrap an arm around Candice's torso, then hold her head against my shoulder with my palm on her forehead. Lovely leans over with a marker pen and draws some squiggles and dots on Candice's face.

"You OK?" I ask her under my breath. She gives me a smile, although it doesn't quite reach her eyes. "Look, my brother is an idiot."

She barks out a laugh, "Rhodie, we both know your brother isn't an idiot. He's the Pres and he has a lot of responsibilities. I won't be a burden on him."

"You're not-"

"Yes, I am. For some reason he sees me as a damsel in distress. I'm not you know, but there's no convincing him otherwise."

I nod. Marx is a stubborn asshole when he wants to be. I open my mouth to say something to make her feel better, but stop when she places a hand on the forearm that's wrapped around Candice.

"I'm fine, Rhodie. I've walked through hell and come out the other side. All this-" she waves her hand around. "All this is cake, as Ana says." She grins at me and I know for a fucking fact

81

that if Marx lets this woman slip through his fingers he'll regret it for the rest of his life. Lovely, the way she is, her strength, her empathy, the way she has Marx in knots? That's first lady shit right there.

Lovely turns to see that Chewy is ready and chomping at the bit to get this phase of her plan started.

"Let's start with 7ml to the top lip."

Chapter 9

Chewy

"What did she say?" Remy asks, brow furrowed.

"I think she said 'Tito dent awol'," Ana shrugs.

"That doesn't make any sense."

"No, she said 'Tito hornors home'," Mira says.

"That makes even less sense!" Blanche says, throwing her hands up. "That's it, I'm dissolving this filler so we can understand her." She waddles toward Pops who hands over a syringe.

Looking at Candice I have to admit, 7ml probably was a *little* too much. That and the amount of wine we gave her makes it almost impossible to understand what the hell she's saying.

"Little too much, huh?" Rhodie asks with the smirk that never ceases to make me wet.

"Maybe, just a teensy bit," I hold my thumb and forefinger apart just a little bit.

I look at Candice's face at the same time Rhodie looks down at her. I take in her huge top lip. It's almost three times the size it once was, and is an interesting shade of purple around the edges. Blanche looks over her shoulder at me, asking permission I think, so I nod in her direction. I mean, it's not like you can fuck up removing filler. Blanche moves to stick the needle in, and a laugh escapes me when I notice that she is using the largest gauge needle we own. Candice must see it too, as she starts to fight against Rhodie. Hard.

"Stay still you silly bitch!" Blanche growls, gripping her cheeks, as she presses the needle into Candice's lip and depresses the plunger.

"Whoa! That looks worse than before," Remy whispers in awe.

My head tilts to the side and I have to admit, it's definitely bigger than it was. "Blanche, did you use the right stuff?"

"I used whatever Pops gave me." She frowns down at the syringe in her hand.

As a collective, we all turn to stare at Pops who is standing with his back to us as he preps my tools.

"Pops?" Blanche growls.

He turns, wide-eyed. He's going for the innocent look. "Whoopsy?"

"Dammit, Pops! Now we really won't know that the hell she's saying," Vi moans.

As if to prove a point Candice says something. I think. It sounds more like mooing.

"See?" Nat waves her hands in the air in a circle, indicating the mooing woman in the chair.

"Shit, keep your hair on girlies," Pops rolls his eyes, and then stomps over.

In the blink of an eye he sticks a needle into Candice's giant purple lip and injects. She squeals and then starts to sob when Pops very roughly starts squishing her lips.

"It's like watching that Dr Pimple Popper woman," Mira whispers to Nat who nods, eyes glued to the scene.

Weird stuff starts oozing out and it kinda is like watching Dr Pimple Popper. At some point Candice goes limp and the whole room freezes, then carries on like nothing ever happened.

"So, all we know is that she was working a front for the cartel," Blanche says.

"Less the cartel, and more this Tito guy. From what I can find he's cartel-adjacent," Remy says, looking up from her laptop.

"What the fuck does that mean?" Rhodie asks.

"Well, he's not working directly for them. I've asked Wire to search the dark web, but I bet Roman knows something," Remy shrugs.

"Pops, you got anything to wake this bitch up? Get this show back on the road?" Blanche asks, hands on hips.

"Is it me or is she crazier than usual?" Rhodie whispers, causing a shiver down my spine as his breath brushes my outer ear.

"No, she's definitely worse than usual," I whisper back, sliding my arm around his waist and leaning into him.

"Here you go, girl, give this a little shake, take the lid off and wave it under the bitch's nose," Pops says, tossing the smelling salts Blanche's way.

She follows his instructions and Candice sits straight up, coughing and spluttering, lips flapping all over the place. It then takes 0.3 seconds for the scent to hit the rest of the room.

"Holy shit! Why is that so strong?" Rhodie asks, covering his nose with his hand, coughing.

"It's my special recipe," Pops replies calmly, a mask over his face.

"Close the lid, Blanche! Holy shitballs!" Vi yells.

Blanche is standing in the middle of the room, her hand outstretched, the scent of the salts permeating the air. My keen sense of smell is being inundated with ammonia and eucalyptus, eyes watering so badly I can barely see. There's a commotion and a pop, then the sounds of something running down the drain underneath Candice's chair.

"Aw shit!" Blanche mumbles.

"What's happening?" Nat shouts, "I can't see anything, my eyes are burning!"

"Fuck!" Rhodie growls, he leaves my side, moving toward where Blanche was standing, "Pops, get that shit covered up and toss the fucker!"

There's rustling and the sound of the door opening and closing.

"Blanche, it's going to be OK," Rhodie's voice says gently.

"I know it's going to be OK! I'm just pissed that I can't fucking see or breathe out of my nose!" she yells back. I let out a sigh, I can hear everyone around me so I know they're all alright and haven't been poisoned by Pops. Perhaps I shouldn't have encouraged him to add more eucalyptus.

"Everyone else alright?" Rhodie asks.

Yeses ring out around the room, Candice says something and I think it's Lovely's voice that tells her to shut up.

"OK, let's get you out of here. Vi? Can you please let Tav know that his baby is on the way?"

"Wait, what?" I ask, blinking my eyes to clear them.

Rhodie has Blanche gently by the elbow, her grey stretchy pants have a large wet patch on the front. Oh, so that's where the water sound came from.

"Holy shit Blanche is having her baby!" Mira yells and all of a sudden the room is full of activity.

I know Marx asked me to get rid of Candice so I'll need to do that before we head out to the hospital.

"Let go! We need to finish this!" Blanche says, snatching her elbow away from Rhodie's hold.

"Umm, shouldn't we be heading out?" Rhodie asks, looking confused as hell.

"Not til we're done," Blanche says in a low voice.

"Filler me!" she says, hand out, waiting for another syringe.

"Blanche," Lovely coos in a gentle voice, as if talking to a scared baby deer, "Are you sure you really want to do this?"

Blanche turns a cold look her sister's way and Lovely stands her ground, hands on her hips. They stare each other down, and I'm impressed at Lovely's ability to not blink for a very long time. I skirt around them both, picking up the filler syringe on the metal table. Uncapping it, I whisper "bye bye" to Candice and then lean in pulling the skin of her neck taut, just under her jaw until I locate the external carotid artery. Finding the perfect spot I press the needle into her neck, waiting for the skin to give way, then sliding it further still, letting it nestle just where I want it.

"There it is," I whisper, then depress the plunger filling the artery with enough filler to cause a blockage. Stroke will happen in a few moments.

"Where is she?" Tav bursts through the doors just as Candice's face starts to droop on the left side.

"I'm here, but I'm not done yet! We need to rid the world of this awful bitch." Blanche indicates Candice whose mouth is now slack, drool running down her chin. "She has to pay for all the shit she put those women through, and all those sweet babie- ow, ow, ow!"

Tav doesn't say a word, just stomps up to his Ol Lady and

scoops her up in her arms. "You good, Dayz?"

Tilting my head I take in Candice's slack features and the blue tinge of her overblown lips. I mean, it's kinda hard to really get a good bead on them, given that they're still purple in places but the hemorrhaging in her eyes tells a different story.

"Yeah, I'm good. Let's roll out."

Rhodie

We follow Tav into the common room so we can rally the troops. Well, that was the plan until Blanche growled at everyone to wait here and give her a two hour head start. Apparently she'd rather we be bored here than staring at the white walls of the hospital while Tav's kid gets ready to meet the world. I'm not sure why she thinks this, but she's said numerous times that Tav's kid will take their time being born. I know nothing about having a baby, so maybe she knows something I don't.

"So, what do we do now?" Mira asks, at a loss now that we're just sitting here.

"Bets! What kind, how heavy and time of birth. Who's in?" Rider booms, holding up a notebook, pen at the ready.

The brothers start yelling out weights and gender, but Chewy just snuggles into me, Laney-May in her lap after Mad Dog handed her over. She's already in her PJ's and Mama Debs assured us that she's been fed, bathed and will be ready for bed whenever we decide. We still haven't fallen into the perfect routine yet, but I think we're bloody close enough. Laney is happy and healthy and seems comfortable here with our family.

"Come on Laney, let's get you and Chomper to bed, hmm?" Chewy softly says, moving to stand. Laney shakes her head roughly, gripping onto Chewy's shirt as she grumbles. "Yup, bed time for you, let's go." Laney fights even harder, first flopping back and almost toppling Chewy over to then going completely rigid as a loud yell leaves her little body.

She rocks back and forward, yelling "No!" at the top of her lungs and Chewy freezes. I rush to get up, to hold them both steady, Laney's rocking and throwing her body around getting more and more unruly.

"Come here, Laney-May," I wrap my hand under Laney's arms and lift her into mine, wrapping my arm around her bottom half to try and keep her safe, but her kicking legs and head shaking and yelling is a little hard to control, especially from a little girl who up until now has been so very well behaved. "Hey, hey, shhhhh, shhhh. It's OK, baby girl, I got you," She throws her head into my shoulder and cries, her tears soaking into my cut.

"She's a bit overtired I think," Mama Debs says gently, giving Chewy a squeeze. "It's been a big day, full of excitement. She'll calm down and probably fall asleep as soon as you put her to bed."

I give her a weak smile, then wrap my free arm around Chewy, pulling her into my side and squeezing. I know this would have overwhelmed her so I'll need to care for my woman as well as my baby.

"If you need me to walk her, let me know," Mad Dog offers, with a nod. Judging by my face, I'm sure he can tell I have no idea what he's talking about. "When you were a kid you were just like her. Wanted to see everything, be everywhere, not wanting to nap. By the evening you were a little shit, you'd shake yourself to stay awake, scream, cry, kick. Anything to not have to go to bed. I'd walk up and down the hall with you until you fell asleep on my shoulder." He shrugs, and I'm so fucking grateful we have all these people to help raise Laney. I'm the fucking luckiest bastard in the world.

"Come on, little mama," I whisper to Chewy, who is still wide-eyed, looking terrified.

We make our way into our room and in the short walk from the common room to here Laney has gotten heavier in my arms. Her head is lolling on my shoulder and her little arms are hanging slackly by her sides. I move silently to her bed, and Chewy moves up to peel the blanket back so I can lie our girl down.

"There you go, baby girl. Shhhhh, daddy and mommy are here." I rub a hand down her back, up and down until her breathing deepens even more. "I think we did it, little ma-" turning, Chewy is no longer at my side. "Babe?"

Looking around the room I notice the closet door is ajar, so I move toward the crack. Sliding to the floor I lean against the wall, letting my head loll to one side so I can see Laney. I watch our daughter, her chest rising and falling gently, little breaths puffing out between her slack lips. The door cracks open a little, but I sit, a strong silent presence to my woman who needs to get her thoughts in order.

Rustling has me turning toward the door to find Gus, Jules and Pops in the doorway. I tip my chin and they move quietly into the room, Mama Debs bringing up the rear. They all find a place on the floor. Gus moves to the wall on the other side of the closet, Mama Debs and Pops lean against the bed and Jules sits, back straight and legs crossed just on the outside of the circle we've made. After a moment more people arrive. Ol ladies, brothers, anyone and everyone we hold dear are all crammed into our room, quietly supporting Chewy as she finds her peace after the overwhelm.

I'm not sure how long we all sit, some of us on our phones, others just with our thoughts. Marx is leaning against the far wall, arms crossed over his large chest. His gaze keeps darting to Lovely who is sitting all prim and proper on the bed. I know he has to be feeling like shit after what he said about Lovely, but fuck, he needs to sort that out and fast. A woman like Lovely won't wait around forever.

"Why are you all here?" Chewy says quietly, standing in the doorway of the closet, her gaze bouncing around the room.

"We're here for you, babe."

"But why?" She searches the room again, "You'd be better off supporting Rhodie." Her brows pinch as she stares at her fingers, "He's the one that needs support. He's a good father and I'm, I'm-"

"Don't fucking say it, girl," Pops growls, everyone in the room nodding in agreement with him. "You are a fucking fantastic mom, Tuesday."

"But-"

"No buts," Mama Debs says. "Laney is two years old. All two-year-olds lose their shit."

Chewy's frown deepens.

"It's true. Bee is a little younger than Laney but she refused her daytime nap the other day. She played all day with the kids and then became overtired and overwhelmed and I was up until midnight trying to get her down." Marx's head snaps in Lovely's direction, concern etched on his face. "She screamed and fought and bit and I felt like the worst mom in the world," Lovely says. "Then she finally went down and when she woke up the next morning she was full of smiles and my world was right again."

"This shit happens, Chewy, it doesn't mean you're a crappy mom," Nat adds in, snuggling Rosie in her arms.

"But, I'm her *mom*. I should know this stuff." Chewy squishes her bottom lip between her thumb and forefinger.

"You've been a mom for a week, baby girl. You've got time to learn this stuff,"

"And even then you'll probably get it wrong," Flack chuckles, sharing a look with my dad and Pops.

"I don't like being wrong." She scowls at the thought of it.

"Well, get used to it, Dayz," Gus says. "In the meantime, we're all here for you."

Her shoulders start to drop and it's magic to watch her realize that she has all these people at her back. Her face relaxes, her brow smoothing out and I know she's about to say something out of pocket when her shoulders pull back. "I'm going to get more efficient at torture and dispatch. I'm a *mom*, I can't spend all night in interrogation. Pops, tomorrow while Laney is having her afternoon nap you and I will do some research. We need fast, efficient ways to interrogate and then get rid of."

Pops grins and nods "It's a date, baby girl,"

"Yes. But after Laney's nap. We can't have her getting overtired again. It probably puts stress on her brain and her learning won't be as effective." She nods once and moves over to look at Laney in her crib. She tugs the blanket up a little, to cover Laney's shoulders and then runs a hand over her curls. "Mama's gonna learn everything I need to know to love you the way you need. Promise."

I smile softly at my woman, and then nod at our family as they all quietly leave, one by one. Moving to stand behind Chewy, I wrap her in my arms as she leans into my chest.

"I love you, Tuesday Tombs. I can't imagine anyone else I'd

want to have by my side."

"I'd never do this with anyone else," Chewy huffs out. "I love you too, Rhodes Paxton. I know it's soon, but I'm pretty sure I love Laney too. When I look at her it makes my chest hurt, right here," she lifts my hand and places it in the middle of her chest, over her heart. "Do you think that's normal?"

"I think that's exactly how we're meant to feel."

She nods, her wild hair tickling my jaw, "It's scary, but I like it."

"Me too, baby. Me too."

Chapter 10

Chewy

This is infernal. Sage offered to look after all the babies so the rest of the MC could be here waiting for Tav's baby. Well, almost the whole MC. Chef decided to stay back and help Sage.

"I think Blanche was right. Tav's baby is going to be slow getting outta there," Nat says, snuggling into Savage.

"I don't get it. Tav is always on time. Mostly he's early," I say to no one in particular.

"Unless he's with Blanche. That man is reluctant to leave that woman. His kid sounds the same," Gus says.

Well, when he puts it like that.

"You doing OK, babe?" Rhodie asks, leaning his chin on the top of my head.

I nod, wiggling his head with my movement. I am good. Better than good. I feel all full up. Not too sure with what. It could be love, perhaps. All I know is that I feel content. Happy. Like there's nothing else in the world for me to want. Oh, other than solving this whole Tito mystery. So far Wire has found that

Tito is a free agent of sorts. He hires himself out to the highest bidder, which for the last decade or so has been the Cordoza family. Marx confirmed that Roman did take out the cartel, leaving the youngest son alive as he doesn't get rid of children. Which seems awfully nice of him, given he's Bratva and all.

My thoughts continue to drift, as does my gaze. I let it run over my family, both by blood and by choice. Judge is even grumpier and quieter than usual. I know he has history with the diner lady, but I have a feeling it's a miscommunication. Humans are so bad at communicating efficiently. Wait, no, it's not all humans. Just the neurotypical ones. Always hiding their thoughts and feelings. It must be exhausting. Judge stands up and paces the floor, stretching his long legs out before slumping back down into his chair. Tank murmurs something to him and I don't even try to read his lips. Hopefully Tank can help Judge out because I'm not sure how long he can stay this tightly wound before he explodes.

Speaking of, Marx seems out of sorts. I wonder if it has something to do with Lovely but she seems like her usual self. Bustling around checking in on everyone, little Bee strapped to her front even though she's huge now. Something is going on there but I can't quite put my finger on it.

"Why do you think your brother acts all weird around Lovely?" I murmur to Rhodie.

My body shakes a little in Rhodie's lap as he chuckles. "You noticed that, huh?"

"Of course I did. I notice everything. It's my super power."

"Well, does your superpower have a romance radar?"

I frown up at Rhodie, "Why would it?"

"The reason Marx acts weird around Lovely is because he wants her but he thinks he can't have her." Rhodie looks at his brother, a smirk on his face.

"Wait, why does he think he can't have her? She's right there."

"Because, my little menace, he doesn't think he deserves her. He thinks he's too old or too dirty or too fucked up or who knows what else he thinks," Rhodie shrugs, jiggling me again.

"Normal people are so confusing," I huff out.

"Oh, says the most complicated, confusing woman I've ever met." Rhodie teases me. I let that one slide. He's probably right. Rhodie is a simple man. He likes simple things and he's landed with me. Poor guy.

"Ladies and gentleman, please allow me to introduce my daughter, Tess January Tombs," Tav beams, holding up a pink, angry looking bundle.

I stare at the baby for a moment before her name sinks in. Tess. Like my mom. My throat feels tight and scratchy and my chest aches with something that feels like it could be heartburn or maybe what happens when you work out too hard. My eyes blink, trying to clear the mist and it's not working. Large, warm arms wrap around me and Rhodie holds me tight. The pressure calming me from the outside in.

"It just hit you, didn't it?" He whispers into my hair. I nod, snuggling closer, my arms folded up T Rex style as I burrow in.

"Dayz? You OK?" Tav's voice is gentle and near, so I turn my head slightly to look at my big brother. "You didn't want to use mom's name did you? Because I can chan-"

"No!" I yell, before taking a breath, "No, no, you use it. I just had forgotten about Mom, it's been so long. And then you came out with Tess and everything got bubbly inside me and the only way it could come out was through my eyeballs," I explain, swiping at my cheeks before leaning forward to take a peek at baby Tess.

My breath catches, she looks just like my mom. Where the rest of us are all dark haired, dark eyed and light brown, Mom was fair with dark hair and blue eyes. Tav's baby has the same coloring. Although, I mean, due to genetics she could get the dark hair and pale skin from Blanche. And babies' eyes change color so really she could look like no one in our family. But does that even matter? Laney isn't really related to us and looks like me and Rhodie. Tess belongs to Tav and Blanche and can look however she wants, she'll still be family.

I reach out a finger and run it down her tiny hand. "She looks just like Mom, Tav. She deserves her name too."

I must say the right thing because the worry in Tav's eyes disappears and he grins big. "Thanks Dayz. I love you, little sis." He whisks the baby away and I lean back into Rhodie, squishing my lip.

"You did good, baby," Rhodie says. "You OK though?"

I think about it for a moment, and even though I feel full up of love or whatever, I'm feeling a little out of sorts and I think I know why. "I'm not OK. I've had too many emotions lately."

"You worried you're getting soft?" Rhodie teases.

"Yes! That's exactly it. Come on, I need to get back to the old me. Let's go dispose of Candice. That will help me until we have a new bad guy to work over."

"Come on then, babe. Lets get rid of Candice, cuddle Chomper, watch Laney sleep, and then I'll fuck you all dirty until you feel like yourself again."

Grinning at him I drop a kiss on his lips. "Let's blow this joint."

Rhodie

I relax back into the couch, the leather creaking under my weight as I watch my woman bustle around the Rev Room. There's needles and empty vials on the stainless steel table she uses for her tools and Candice Rogers' body exactly where we left it when Blanche went into labor. Neither of us are bothered though. In fact, leaving her for these past few hours has actually been helpful. Any piss she had in her is now down the drain. I mean, it won't help with any shit she may have in her pants, but I'm sure Chewy doesn't mind.

Chewy stands between Candice and her storage cupboard, looking at one, then the other.

"Need a hand babe?" I call out.

"I'm not sure whether I want to go with dismemberment or a good ol fashioned acid bath. OR something completely new and exciting." Her eyes light up at that, before she frowns again.

"Well, what are the downsides to them all?"

Her face screws up a little as she purses her lips. "Well, dismemberment is always messy and super tiring and then we still have to get rid of the bits. Acid bath is efficient and not as hard to get rid of the waste."

"And the new and exciting way?" I prompt when she doesn't continue.

My Ol Lady's eyes dart around and she starts to fidget. She's done something. "Chewy, what have you done?"

"What? Nothing!" She's still not saying anything so I stand, and cross my arms. She hates when I do that.

"Tuesday Tombs, what have you got planned?"

Her fingers tap their beat frantically before she stares me

straight in the eye and says, "I've bought something."

"Oooookay,"

"Gah! I've bought 200 litres of liquid nitrogen and a chipper." her eyes are wide as she stares at me. I stare back. I mean, she did what?

We stand in silence, the only sound is a weird groan that Candice's body makes, along with the trickling of more piss down the drain.

"You bought 200 litres of liquid nitrogen?" I ask in a hoarse voice. How the fuck did she manage that? I mean, the chipper I understand, they sell those at hardware stores and shit.

"Well, yeah. See, the plan is to use the compressor to spray her body with liquid nitrogen, thus flash freezing her. Then we put her through the chipper and straight onto the veggie garden out back," Chewy says, bouncing a little on her toes like it's the best plan she's had in a long time. It's not terrible.

Then I realize what she's said. "Nope, no way, you can fertilize the trees and shit out back, but not the veggies. Fuck that, I already don't want to eat salad now, I aint eating it if it's got this bitch all over it," I thrust my chin in Candice's direction. "Besides, Mama Debs will kill you."

"Huh," she says, as if it didn't even occur to her that maybe, just maybe sprinkling her victims over the garden patch might be a bad thing. "Well, OK then. Just over the back yard. Happy?"

"Very."

"Good. So, which one do you think we should do?"

A slow smile grows over my face. "Ice and chipper, baby."

* * *

"You know, that was a lot quicker to clean up than I expected." Chewy says, cuddling Chomper to her chest, as we gaze down at Laney, fast asleep in her bed.

After that first night we converted it to a toddler bed, seeing as she's a big girl and all that.

"Yeah. It was pretty fucking cool. Less messy with her being frozen too," I agree.

Her head bobs in my periphery and she drops a kiss to Chomper's snout, dodging his lazy snap. I let out a huff and run my hand over Laney's baby soft hair, sifting it through my fingers. A little smile plays on her lips so I do it again, then crouch, laying my head on her pillow, staring into her sleeping face.

"Daddy loves you, Laney-May. No matter what happens, I'll always be there to kick asses for you."

Chewy runs her fingers through my hair as I gently press a kiss to Laney's forehead. Standing, I gaze down at my woman. The person who came into my life, turned it upside down and somehow made it infinitely better.

"Thank you, baby. It's because of you I have a family of my own." I run my thumb down her soft cheek.

"No, we have a family because of *you*, Rhodie. I wouldn't have been able to do any of the things I've done without you at my side. You make me feel safe and seen and I can be me. Just me. And that means that I can then use all my brainpower to move heaven and earth to give you everything you deserve. Like the perfect gator son and the perfect daughter." She grins up at me and I know that's as flowery as her words will ever be. And they're perfect because they belong to her. "So, are we gonna fuck now?"

Chapter 11

Chewy

"The end." I smile down at the top of Laney's curly head as I close up Yertle the Turtle.

"Argh, so good. Thank fuuu–udgeballs you gave up reading that Lord of the Rings crap. Dr. Seuss is way better," Rider says, snuggled into the beanbag next to me and Laney.

"You're a fully grown man."

"Yeah, a fully grown man who knows how badass Dr. Seuss is. Those rhymes are tight."

I don't answer him. He kinda has a point. As much as I would love Laney to broaden her vocabulary by listening to Lord of the Rings it seems that perhaps it's a little advanced for her at this age. Besides, she seems to really like the Dr. Seuss ones *and* they have social commentary in them so she's still learning. She crawls off my lap and heads toward the blocks, which seem to be her favourite thing to do outside of reading with me. That makes me feel good. Never did I really think I'd enjoy this parenting stuff this much. I guess in my mind all I thought was there was a kid that needed Rhodie and me, and Rhodie would do all the parenting. Instead I have a little girl who I can help shape to be a good person. I mean, it's pretty much all we can do. Take whatever skills we've learned in our lifetimes and use them to make good humans, because there sure are a lot of trash people out there.

Laney's curly head turns toward the door as the sound of children drift down the hall.

"What the heck Laney-girl?" I mutter as I move to the doorway, leaning my head out to hear better.

"Alright children, remember your manners," Jazz's voice drifts out of the common room and a smile tugs on my lips.

I totally forgot today was the day Jazz and her art class would be visiting to draw Pops, Mad Dog and, well, the common room.

"Shi-zz it's the pose off!" Rider jumps up from the beanbag and legs it out of the room.

"Quick, come on Laney, let's go watch." I hold my hand out to her and she takes it immediately.

Smiling down at her, I'm still amazed that this is my kid. It's not been all plain sailing, however. After that first meltdown where we both spiralled, she's had a few more moments like that. Instead of it freaking me out like the first time, we've managed to find a way that works for both of us. Meaning, we both end up in the dark cosiness of the closet.

"Go co'room?" Laney asks, looking up at me.

She's started saying a few things here and there. Rhodie is really good at narrating what he's doing, as that's what the literature says we should do to encourage speech, but I still struggle. If I'm doing something then I'm busy in my head concentrating on that one thing. So I do forget to tell her what I've got going on, and to be honest, half the time I'm not exactly sure what I've got going on because my brain works so fast.

That's usually when I get overwhelmed, because I worry I'll get locked in to something and neglect Laney.

"Co'room?" Laney says again, tugging on my hand.

Her hand is a little moist, so it snaps me out of my thoughts, but in a good way. "Yup, Laney-May. We're going to the common room,"

"Yay!" She throws her free hand up in the air and her feet try to run all while holding my hand. She isn't very fast, but she can't really help that I guess. Her legs are pretty short.

We stop in the mouth of the hall and peek in. I don't really want to be in here if there are too many children and too many noises. Usually I'd draw the line at all the smells too, as children usually smell, but it's a given that the art class will stink. Children always smell like outside and wet pennies. So far I can only see around a dozen kids, all in various states. Rodney is smack back in the middle looking dishevelled, his red hair sticking up all over the place. I don't like him.

Laney makes a noise and moves closer to me, leaning her weight against my leg. Huh, maybe she doesn't like kids? No, that can't be right. She chases after Cove and Jovie and she likes to sit and play with blocks next to Bee, Jr, Rosie and Juno. Maybe she just doesn't like stranger-kids? I really hope that's the case because I don't want to have to make friends with other kids' moms. They're probably all lame. I have my Girl Gang mom group and that's all I need.

Laney lets go of my hand and wraps both her arms around my leg, holding on tight. Non- Mom Chewy would shrug and head back to our room to read or research something. But Mom Chewy has to do mom stuff, so I gently unwrap Laney from me and kneel down to her level. I look into her bright green eyes briefly before settling on her button nose.

"Hey, it's OK," I soothe. "I will be with you the whole time, so you don't need to be scared, OK?" I flick my eyes back to hers so she knows I'm being truthful with her.

Her dark brows are furrowed and her eyes dart to the big kids and back to mine. I cuddle her to me before setting her back, and looking at her once more.

"If any of those kids pick on you I'll make sure to make them pay. I won't beat the snot out of them or anything, but I'll become their and their parents' worst nightmare."

Because my kid is the cleverest toddler there is, she understands every word, giving me a huge smile before tugging me into the room and the chaos. Jazz has set the children up on two of the long tables. She teaches special needs so there are some kids with crayons, some with pencils and some with large sponges and paints or with hand braces to help hold their chosen medium.

"This place smells bad," Rodney starts up.

"Rodney, what have I told you? If you don't have anything nice to say..." Jazz prompts.

"But Miss Davies, it *does* stink!" a little blonde girl with wide set eyes and wonky pigtails joins in.

All the other kids start nodding in earnest now and some of the brothers are sniggering behind their hands. It's a work day but it seems that the whole MC has come out to watch the tie breaker to find out who is the best grandpa. Or something. I'm actually not sure why Pops and Mad Dog are doing this.

Laney and I make our way over to the couches to get an uninterrupted view.

"Popcorn?" Mira asks, holding out the bowl, eyes on what's happening in front of us.

"Can Laney eat popcorn?" I ask, brows pinched. I've not

104

gotten this far in my research of foods just yet.

"She'll be fine, *kotiro*, you'll just have to watch her," Mama Debs says, dropping a kiss first on the top of my head then Laney's.

Well, she'd know, so I grab a handful and then pass Laney some kernels. She gobbles them up and then holds her little hand out for more.

"So ladies, who do we think is going to win?" Blanche asks, sitting gingerly next to me.

I eye her up. It's only been two days since Tess was born and I figured she'd still be recovering. Instead she's wearing stretchy pants, looking relaxed. Well, apart from when she stops to bark instructions at three of her older children. Looking around the room my gaze lands on Tav, standing by the bar, Tess strapped to his front. If anyone was made to be a dad, it was that man. Actually, all my brothers were made to be fathers. And I was made to be someone's mom. That someone has her chunky foot resting on my leg, her damp looking hand open and waiting for more popcorn.

"I think Pops will win. Obviously," I reply, handing over three big fluffy popcorns.

Vi joins our Ol Lady circle, taking a seat on the floor. "Trust me, neither of them will win. The only winners here are those feral kids of Jazz's."

"Vi! They're only children!" Remy scolds.

"No, they're not. They're demons disguised as children. Trust me."

We all look over, the kids all sitting nicely at the common room tables ready to get started.

"Macaroni Cheese!"

"Everybody freeze!" The kids yell out in reply to Jazz.

"Right, everyone, welcome to the Devil's Rose Clubhouse! Marx –" Jazz waves to the Pres, "– was nice enough to let us come and draw here, and how exciting! Look around, there is, um, artwork on the walls, and motorcycle parts and things." Jazz's hands wave around the room and the kids sit there, unimpressed.

"Hey! I know you! You were my doctor that time!" a little boy in a motorized wheelchair calls out, pointing at Switch.

"That's right, I remember you, Marcus," Switch booms. "How's your mom?"

Marcus's eyes behind his large glasses narrow, "Why do you want to know? Are you some kind of creep?"

Snorts sound out around the clubhouse while Switch's jaw drops.

"Marcus! We don't talk to people like that, especially to doctors," Jazz scolds. "Right, let me introduce you to our two lovely models who are posing for us today! We have Pops," Pops steps forward and gives the kids the stink eye, "and Mad Dog."

"Mad Dog? What sort of name is *that*?" Rodney yells out.

"And so it begins," Vi whispers."

"That's a good question, son," Mad Dog starts.

"I'm not your son, you're lying!" Rodney shouts.

"Rodney, remember that sometimes people will use other names when they don't know your real name. Like how some people call me Miss, or people get called Doctor, that sort of thing." Jazz patiently explains. This is good stuff. I can use this when Laney gets older.

"Your teacher is right, I mean no harm," Mad Dog smiles. "Mad Dog is a road name. That's the name bikers go by."

"Wait, so you're in a club with other old men and you just give each other nicknames?" Rodney asks, causing the brothers to snicker.

"Well, um, not quite," Mad Dog mumbles.

Pops stands with a huge grin on his face. He hasn't had to put up with any remarks, so he'll be loving that Mad Dog is in the hot seat.

"Oookay, well enough about that. Let's get started shall we?" The kids all nod and Pops and Mad Dog start swinging their arms around, as if limbering up a little. Jazz shakes a coffee cup and then pulls a piece of paper from it, unfurling it and reading aloud "Two men rock climbing. Oh, that's easy enough."

Pops and Mad Dog arrange themselves, arms up, fingers curled as if on a rockface.

The cute little blonde girl raises her hand and asks if Pops could put his foot up on a chair, so he looks like he's really climbing. The scrape of wooden chair legs breaks through the chatter and Pops hoists his chino's a little higher, then stomps his foot onto the seat of the chair.

"Oohhh, that's good! Maybe get that other Dog guy to stand behind him!" A little boy with the name tag "Buddy" says.

Mad Dog does as requested, standing behind Pops, then raising his arms.

"Ew! He's got wet patches under his arms!" yet another little boy calls out.

"No no no!" The blonde wonky pigtailed girl starts chanting, "I don't want to grow up and have crying armpits like them!"

"Now, Sophie, we've been over this," Jazz soothes and I'm mesmerized by her skills. "Remember, that some people sweat more than others, and you can avoid wet patches like that by wearing antiperspirant," she smiles, looking at all the kids.

"I swear Mad Dog is blushing," Ana snorts under her breath.

"OK, kids, let's turn our concentration brains back on. Thank you Pops and Mad Dog for posing for us," Jazz says, getting this car crash back on track.

"Miss Jasmine, maybe the sweaty dog man can hold on to the back of the old man, like he's holding onto him so he doesn't fall!" Buddy says, the other kids "oohing" over his suggestion.

Pops scowls at Mad Dog as he gently grips him, hands on either side of his waist.

Snapping my gaze back to the kids I notice Elio frowning at the scene in front of him, his pencil poised above his paper. His gaze meets mine and my newfound positive mom vibes make me smile and give him a thumbs up. He frowns even deeper before turning back to the front of the common room.

The little blonde girl with wonky pigtails tugs on Jazz's sweater. "Could the dog man maybe put his foot on the chair too and lean back a little? It'll look really actiony and scary," she says in a whisper, and then grins at the "scary" part. Clearly over her little meltdown about growing up to be sweaty.

Tittering sounds out around me and the Ol Ladies try hard not to laugh at what's happening. The brothers aren't as discreet, all of them have their phones out, recording.

"Gentlemen? Did you hear Sophie's request?"

"Just fucking do it," Pops hisses under his breath, quietly, but not quietly enough so as not to be heard.

"Miss Jasmine! He said a swear!" the wheel chair boy calls out, looking scandalized.

"Sorry I upset you, kid," Pops mumbles at him.

"I'm not upset, just disappointed."

Pops stares at him then glares over his right shoulder at Mad Dog, "Just get this over with. It's for the kids."

Mad Dog shoves him a little, kicking Pops' Skechers loafer with his big black boot, his and Pops feet both up on the chair.

"That's it!" One of the kids calls out excitedly, "Now lean back just a little!"

Mad Dog leans back a little, hands on Pops waist to keep himself steady.

"Oh. Oh no."

Rhodie

We all see it at the same time. There, in front of a dozen special needs kids, the MC brothers and all the Ol Ladies; my father and my grandfather-in law are posed as lovers. By "lovers" I mean that it looks like Mad Dog is fucking Pops.

"We are all seeing this, right?" Rider asks. He's my oldest friend. I know all his moods and voices and I know for a fucking fact this is the sound of him repressing his laughter.

One look at him and I know the both of us will burst into giggles and we'll get our asses whooped. Well, Mad Dog will whip our asses. Pops will flash freeze us and throw our giggly asses in the chipper.

"Do you think we should tell them?" Lovely whispers, eyeing the men. Shit, if sheltered Lovely can recognise the pose, then anybody can. Apart from the two men at the front of the room.

"Miss Jasmine, can the man in front lean forward? There's a glare on his big forehead and I can't draw it," a cute little redheaded girl whines.

Pops takes his cue and leans forward at the waist. A guffaw bursts out, my head snapping around to find Dex with his hand slapped over his mouth. Fuck, even Sniper, the most stoic brother we have, has his lips rolled between his teeth. Switch, being a ginger, has turned dangerously red from holding in his laughter and Rider is silently rolling on the floor, a wheeze escaping him periodically. Fuck. Do I tell them? Not if I want to live. I catch Marx's eye and widen mine at him, then dart them to the men at the front of the room. My brother frowns, mouthing "What?" at me, so I tip my head in the direction of the old couple at the front.

Marx moves from his position near the kitchen hatch, closer to where I'm standing and I see the exact moment he sees it. His head snaps in my direction, eyes huge as he mouths "What. The. Fuck?" I shrug, trying hard not to laugh at the look on his face. I know he probably wants to piss himself too, but he's the Pres so at least one of us has to pull themselves together.

"Ah, Jazz?" he coughs, clearing his throat. "Can I have a word?"

Jazz quickly surveys the kids before moving quietly beside Marx. He leans down, murmuring to her. Her dark head turns to look at the scene, then she spins toward Marx, her hands over her mouth. She's not devastated or embarrassed. No, judging by her shoulders shaking she's laughing.

"Um, Dog man, can you please get lower?" A woman who came in with a deaf little girl asks, nodding at the girl as her hands fly, making shapes in the air.

Dad squats down a little lower, but because of the positioning he looks even more mid- thrust than he did before. "Like this?"

The woman looks down at the dark haired girl who grins and puts two thumbs up, before picking up her pencil and getting back to work. I turn back to the car crash happening in front of me just in time to see Pops shove his ass back, unsteadying Mad

Dog.

"Stop gripping me so fu-reaking tight," Pops growls.

"Shut it, Pops. This pose is killing me!"

"Pussy!" Pops hisses.

"Where? I love pussies!" One of the kids shouts out, then gets up, moving around the room yelling "Pussy! Puuuuuu-ussssssyyy!"

Rider lets out an even higher pitched wheeze from his place on the floor. Fuck, even the Ol Ladies are doubled over on the couch. Mira has her face buried in a cushion, Ana is snorting like a pig, Remy's shoulders are shaking violently even though no noise is coming out and there, in the chaos sits my Ol Lady, looking perplexed.

Mad Dog's legs start dangerously shaking and I know that he can't hold that pose all day. But looking at Pops, he's not doing much better. He's on one leg, bent forward, ass out.

"Ugh, I can't draw the old man's camel toe!" some kid whines before tossing their pencils with such flair that it's almost impressive.

"Dwayne! You clean up your mess right now!" Jazz says in a firm voice, trying everything to not look at the scene in front of her.

"TIIIMBER!" That orange kid Rodney yells just as Pops and Mad Dog topple in a heap on the ground.

"Ow! Your goddamn belt buckle is digging into me!" Pops grumbles, wriggling around on the floor.

"It's not my belt buckle," Mad Dog grits out.

Pops freezes, wide eyed before turning and trying to punch my Dad. There are gasps from the children before Rodney yells "Fight!" then it's all on. The kids start chanting "Fight, fight, fight!" while banging on the table. There are howls of laughter as the brothers and Ol Ladies finally let it all out, and Marx stands pinching his brow.

"There! Finished!" A cute little blonde girl with Downs Syndrome says, holding up her picture.

"Holy shi-rt," Rider catches quickly, "That's really good sweetheart."

She picks it up and skips over to Pops and Mad Dog who are still tussling on the floor. "Excuse me Mr Old Man and Mr Dog Man, but do you like my drawing of you?"

They both stop rolling around so they can sit up and look at her picture. The soft smiles on their faces freeze in place as their eyes widen.

"Oh, um, is that us?" Mad Dog asks, trying to keep his reaction in check.

She nods enthusiastically and both Pops and Mad Dog shower her with compliments until she races off to show it to her teacher.

"Holy fuck," Pops whispers. "We're going to have to make Jazz burn those."

"Fuck yes," Mad Dog agrees.

Pops nods vigorously, not stopping, I think he's in shock. "Look, I think everybody has a right to love who they want to love. In saying that, I will destroy every picture in existence of you posing like you're bumming me."

Pops and my dad share a look. "Deal. I don't want that shit getting out either."

They nod once, then Pops stands, holding his hand out to help Dad up. As Dad gets to standing, Pops pulls him in close. "Just so you know, I'm number one Pops." Mad Dog goes to open his mouth but Pops cuts him off, "You can be number one Doggy."

Dad grins wide, shaking Pops' hand and tipping his chin.

"Deal."

I decide I've had enough of this circus. Chewy must think the same. As soon as she looks at me she grins, whispers to Laney and they both stand. Laney-May comes running so I scoop her up, spinning her around before settling her on my forearm. Chewy reaches me not long after, wrapping her arms around my waist.

"Well, that was chaos," I say to Chewy, leading her out of the common room.

"Yeah. I still don't know who won," Chewy says, looking perplexed.

"I think it ended in a tie. Also, remind me to never ask Jazz to bring her kids anywhere near me. They're fucking brutal."

Chewy's tinkling laugh rings out, "Oh, so fucking brutal! I thought Pops was going to have a conniption when they said he had a camel toe," she giggles before sobering. "I'm glad that it's a tie. Laney has lots of room in her heart for two grandpas. That's how hearts work, they grow," Chewy says matter of factly.

"That they do, baby."

We move into our suite, and I put Laney down on the floor. She toddles over to her little corner, filled with toys and books and her blocks. Oh, and Chomper, who moves slowly toward her. He's good with her, waiting for her to sit before he takes his place at her side. She leans her body against his and picks up her first block, placing it in front of her just so.

"What have you lost?" she asks, noticing me looking around the room.

"Laney's gator stuffy. Have you seen it?"

Chewy's brows furrow. We move around the room looking in her bed and in the bathroom. The sound of Jazz's voice drifts in from outside as she herds her art class into the waiting bus, Lovely helping her with the stragglers.

"That's so weird," Chewy murmurs. "She never goes anywhere without it."

I nod, she's right. Since the night Chewy brought her home she's been glued to her stuffy. Well, she was. I can't actually remember the last time I saw her with it.

"Shit, what do we do? Do we buy a new one and pretend it's the same one?" I ask, feeling a little frantic. What happens when my little girl realizes it's gone? What if she gets upset and we can't calm her down?

Chewy and I frantically start googling gator stuffies, not even noticing Mama Debs coming in and watching us until she lets out a giggle.

"Whatcha doing you two?" she asks, a twinkle in her eye.

"Fuck, we've lost Laney's gator stuffy, so we're trying to find another one to replace it before she notices she doesn't have it," I explain.

Mama Debs looks toward Laney, then her gaze moves elsewhere before coming back to mine, a smile playing on her lips. "*Tama*, I don't think she needs that gator stuffy anymore, she has the real thing," she tips her head toward Laney and there, in her lap, her little hand running from the top of his head, to the bottom of his tail, is Chomper, soaking up the affection.

Chewy lets out a gasp, her hand landing on my forearm to steady herself. "Rhodie! She doesn't need her stuffy, she has us, and her gator brother!"

I grin at my girl, then my woman, then Mama Debs.

"She's perfect for you two. It's almost like she sent Dima to find you, and not the other way around." Mama Debs winks before leaving the room.

"Perfect," Chewy whispers., "You're perfect for me and she's perfect for us." My Ol Lady turns to me, eyes bright, "Perfect."

I press my lips to hers, and then the world goes dark.

Epilogue

Marx

It's chaos. It's motherfucking chaos. One moment we were laughing with each other in the common room, giving Dad and Pops shit, and then next minute bullets ring out and half the fucking roof caves in. I shake my head, trying to rid myself of the screams of terror from the Ol Ladies and the MC kids. Once the memory of their voices clears the memory of the blood, so much blood permeates my mind.

"Pres?" Nitro's voice breaks through my thoughts, taking my mind off the fucking hard chair I'm sitting in.

I bolt upright from my chair, wanting to know, no, *needing* to know how Fox is doing.

"He's stable. They're going to leave him in an induced coma for another couple of days to let him heal ..." he trails off.

I grip his shoulder, giving it a gentle squeeze. "Thanks Nitro, now go look after your man."

He gives me a look, almost shocked that I could see what hadn't even occurred to him until the moment Fox took two to the gut. Nitro swallows, his adam's apple bobbing as he tries to find the words.

"I can't lose him, Pres," he blinks moisture from his eyes.

"I know, and you won't. Now get back there and make sure he knows you'll kick his ass if he doesn't wake up soon." He gives me a chin lift before turning to leave the room.

"Pres? You do the same for Lovely, yeah?" My eyes dart to the person in the bed behind me, before meeting Nitro's gaze. I give him a single nod, and he leaves, walking through the doors to Lovely's room.

Sitting heavily back down in the chair I let my gaze run over the woman lying before me. Gentle. Kind. Infuriating. Brave. Lovely.

A knock breaks me out of my thoughts and I snap to attention again, my men, no, my family need me.

"Come in," I call out, waiting to see who it is this time.

"Just me," Rhodie says, leading Pops and Mad Dog into the room. He swallows, looking at Lovely. "How is she?" I just shake my head. Her condition hasn't changed since she came out of surgery, but it's early days yet. He nods in understanding. "The clubhouse will be a complete rebuild."

Fuck. I lean forward in my chair, scrubbing my hands down my face. Where the fuck are my MC going to go? I open my mouth to bitch about it, but I'm stopped from saying anything at Pops' raised hand.

"I live in a big fucking farmhouse. I'm surrounded by land, and it's private. The MC can have the house until we're back on our feet," he says earnestly.

I stare at him. This pain in my ass has just offered us sanctuary. Pops, who has spent his life winding us up, has selflessly offered up his home.

"Well, fuck, don't go soft on me, kid. You got vengeance to

117

reap."

I'm shocked when a laugh bursts out of me and I let it rumble over me, my shoulders relaxing as one really big fucking problem has now been solved by Sidney Tombs.

"Pops, thank you." My voice breaks at the end but I don't give a shit.

"You're family, kid. Through better or worse."

Mad Dog grips Pops shoulder, giving him a squeeze, then they turn to leave. "We'll sort out the MC. You get the rest of your shit in order," Dad calls over his shoulder.

"Anything you need brother, call me. Chewy and the Computa's have relocated to the Tombs offices. They're working around the clock to find anything of use. Roman called, he and Sasha are bringing in Dima to help."

"Good, that's good." My phone vibrates and I pull it from my cut, glancing at the screen. "Landry's will be here by tonight."

"Fuck," Rhodie's eye's drift to Lovely.

Scrubbing my hand down my face I let out a long breath, "I know brother."

"I'll go help Pops and Dad, get the walking wounded settled and hit the streets with Jules. Someone out there must know something."

I give my little brother a nod, stand and then pull him into my arms. "Be safe out there,"

"Always."

He turns to leave, knocking twice on the door jamb, leaving me alone with the woman who has had me in knots since she first set foot in my clubhouse.

"I know I've been an ass, but listen to me, and listen good," I whisper to her. She doesn't move, not even a flutter of her eyelids, but it doesn't matter, I have to get this out. "Fuck all

118

that shit I said, you're mine. Hear me, Lovely? You. Are. Mine."

Thank you for reading!

Phew! Thank you so much for following along for Chewy's ride, it's always so nice to go back and revisit someone as fun as Chewy.

Please don't forget to drop a review, reviews for authors are like virtual hugs!

If you want to follow me then please drop into any of my groups or social media, I''d love to hear from you!

Friend me on Facebook

Join my group Cleo Browne's Babes

Follow me on Instagram

Cleo Browne Books

Rhodie – Devil's Rose MC Book One

August – A Tombs Security + Devil's Rose MC Crossover

Wire – Devil's Rose MC Book Two

Tav Devil's Rose MC Book Three
DRMC – Devil's Rose Merry Christmas

Tank – Devil's Rose MC Book Four

Jules – A Tombs Security + Devil's Rose MC Crossover

Tuesday – Devil's Rose MC Book Five (novella)

Marx – Devil's Rose MC Book Six
In progress

Acknowledgements

First off, I'd like to thank all the wonderful readers who took a chance on a kooky little autistic woman and read my first offering, Rhodie. Without you all reading it and loving it, this book would never have happened. I would have just faded away into obscurity, never to be seen or heard from again. So, thank you. I appreciate you all.

Second, I'd like to thank my book besties who all have a hand in helping me get these stories to you guys, the readers. Thanks to Shaye Torrel for the Book Bitch meet ups, Courtney Clarke Michaels for the speed talk meet ups, Gabi Brocklesby for the proof reading because holy crap, without you these books would be a hard read, and Sally Howells for the AMAZING alpha advice and chapter breakdowns and for always knowing where my weird brain is going to go at any moment. Thank you all from the bottom of my weird little heart.

Thanks to my partner PN. Without his constant words of encouragement, "I really didn't think MC books were a thing," I would never have finished this book. Thanks also go to my boys. Ronnie, for being completely disinterested, and Louis for your two hour long phone calls that would eat into my writing time. Love you guys.